... wonderful tale, told with heart,
hope and a shiny wet nose."
– Gill Lewis, author of *Swan Song*

"A really special book."
– Hilary McKay, author of *The Skylarks' War*

"A story full of humanity."
– Cath Howe, author of *Ella on the Outside*

"Funny, touching and deeply true, it's a story
about the 'red thread' that binds a family together
through illness and change, and the love of a dog."
– Sinéad O'Hart, author of *The Eye of the North*

"A simply perfect book about a boy and his dog
navigating a painfully well-observed imperfect situation...
Funny and warm and ultimately leaves a glow."
– Perdita Cargill, author of *Waiting for Callback*

"Heartbreakingly brilliant! Warm, funny, sad,
tender, with poetry that punches your heart."
– Tamsin Winter, author of *Being Miss Nobody*

"A gorgeous uplifting story about dogs, step-families
and how they come in all shapes and sizes, and
the difference a great teacher can make."
– Rhian Ivory, author of *The Boy Who Drew the Future*

"Warm, funny, kind, heartbreaking in places, but most
of all just so vivid. It'll stay with me for ages!"
– Nicola Penfold, author of *Where the World Turns Wild*

"The story of a young boy who navigates his way through
the tricky territory of family changes and new relationships
with his beloved pet dog. A masterpiece in observation.
Tender, humorous, important."
– Rachel Delahaye, author of *Mort the Meek*

STRIPES PUBLISHING LIMITED
An imprint of the Little Tiger Group
1 Coda Studios, 189 Munster Road,
London SW6 6AW

Imported into the EEA by Penguin Random House Ireland,
Morrison Chambers, 32 Nassau Street, Dublin D02 YH68

www.littletiger.co.uk

First published in Great Britain by Stripes Publishing Limited in 2022
Text copyright © Ros Roberts, 2022
Illustrations copyright © Thy Bui, 2022

All emojis designed by OpenMoji License: CC BY-SA 4.0

ISBN: 978-1-78895-346-7

A CIP catalogue record for this book is available from the British Library.

Printed and bound in the UK.

The Forest Stewardship Council® (FSC®) is a global, not-for-profit
organization dedicated to the promotion of responsible forest management
worldwide. FSC defines standards based on agreed principles for
responsible forest stewardship that are supported by environmental,
social, and economic stakeholders. To learn more, visit www.fsc.org

2 4 6 8 10 9 7 5 3 1

ROS ROBERTS

EVERY CLOUD

LITTLE TIGER

LONDON

For my eldest son – inventor of home sw—

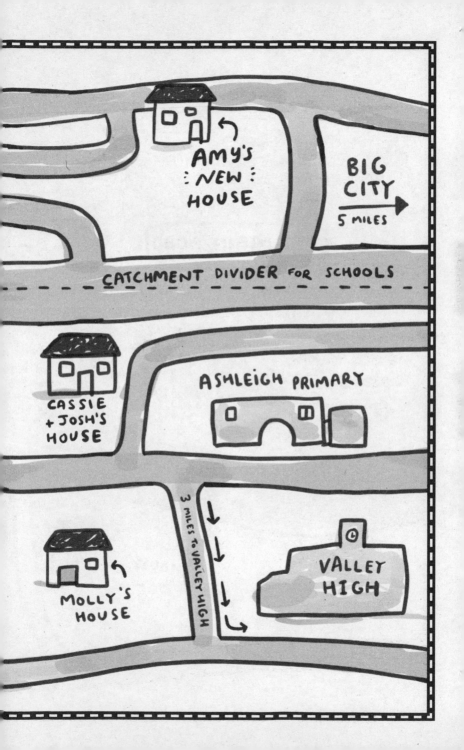

One

"The thing I can't understand," says Cassie, slanting her eyes at me and redoing her ponytail as if she needs to drag this out a bit, "is how you've *got* a place at our high school. I mean, Sophia actually lives *in* the catchment area, right on the edge near the road, and she's only *just* got in. So how can *you* have a place when you're miles away?"

I look down at the playground tarmac and roll my shoe over some loose pebbles.

"Ames used to live in the village," says Molly, resting her head on my shoulder. Her hair smells of peaches. It always does. "Right near me. Surely that's enough, and she goes to Ashleigh, like us. She *has* to come to Valley High."

"I am," I say, shuffling on the bench. "Mum and Dad told me right at the beginning that they would make sure it was all OK."

Cassie shrugs and looks across at the field. "I don't know how, that's all," she says. Molly lifts her head off my shoulder.

I feel her elbow Cassie to make her stop. "Of course I hope you *do* have a place with us," says Cassie. "But the rules are you have to live in the catchment area in October and you moved *ages* ago."

The rules are... Who does Cassie think she is? The prime minister?

"It wasn't ages ago," says Molly.

"It was last summer," I say.

"Oh," says Molly. She turns to me. I'm looking at my shoes but I can feel her staring at me, as if she's just got really worried about it.

"My parents promised," I say quietly, as if I don't quite believe them myself now. "They said when we moved, they would make sure I still got in. Lots of kids go to Valley High from far away."

"Yeah," says Cassie. "But my mum says they've built tons of new houses since then and that changes everything."

I bite my lip. I want to tell Cassie to shut up. *My mum says...* Who is she today? The queen of high school placements?

But I am feeling uneasy in my tummy.

"It'll be hard," says Cassie, jumping off the bench, "for us to stay triple besties if we're not together." She glances at me and Molly, but we just stare ahead and don't say anything.

One of the lunch staff opens the big door and props it open, about to call us in.

"Well, I'm just saying," says Cassie, "you weren't on the list this morning for Wednesday's Year Seven visit. I saw it on Miss Riley's desk." She walks over to the doors and waits with Sophia.

Well, I'm just saying... I mimic under my breath.

"I wish she'd stop with this triple bestie thing," says Molly. "She told Jess the other day that she couldn't hang out with us. It's not right."

"I know," I say and I lean in to her.

"You must be on the list," she says. "Let's ask this afternoon. Come on." But I can't move. I feel sick. I stare at the ground, at my feet. I'm cold all over. Why wasn't I on the list? Last week I gave Mum the letter to order my uniform and it's still on the side, under her diary. Molly showed me her bus pass that arrived yesterday. I don't know anything about a bus.

We walk over to join the others. I don't think I can eat a thing.

"Are you sure you moved in the summer?" asks Molly, her arm wrapped in mine. "I think it was later."

"I'm sure," I say and I remember the removal men, dripping with sweat in the summer heat, coming up to my room to take all my boxes, me tucked in the corner of my bed, staring at the clouds painted on the ceiling for the very last time. Mum promised my new bedroom ceiling would have clouds. Bigger, better, whiter, fluffier clouds but the ceiling is still mucky white and cracked.

"Actually, you're right," says Molly, hugging her packed lunch box to her chest. "We had that sleepover in the new garden before school went back." I nod. "And we came to your house at Halloween, do you remember?"

How could I forget?

"We hid in that cupboard," says Molly, "and scared ourselves silly. And Cassie screamed when the floorboards squeaked." I smile a little, as if I remember it as fun. But it wasn't fun to me. It was horrid. I hated the new house. I still do. It's old and ugly and the shower works in one tiny spurt, like a broken hosepipe.

"It was so fun," says Molly, laughing out loud. "Maxi wore that pumpkin Babygro with the matching hat." I smile at that. He did look super cute. "Remember your mum hung doughnuts on the washing line and we had that race to see who could eat the most? And Sophia won. And then we wrapped your dad in toilet paper, like a mummy. We did his crutches too. And your gran was there, in her giant witch's hat and she made those eyeball cakes!"

I smile and nod and I'm glad Molly has a good memory of that night, even if I don't. I think it was one of the first times we really knew Pops wasn't well. He ate a whole plate of biscuits, every one of them. And then he got really upset at the costumes and noise and Gran had to take him home early, her witch's hat shoved on the back shelf of the car, its pointy top all twisted.

We sit in our usual Year 6 spot. Cassie is up at the counter. We open our packed lunches. Mum's put a note in.

Amy – sorry there's no yoghurt. Love you x

"I wish you hadn't moved away," says Molly.

"Yeah, me too," I say and I take out my tuna wrap and I feel suddenly very tearful thinking about the list of names for Valley High. The list I'm pretty sure my name's not on.

Two

It's nearly a year since we moved but I still hate home time. I still hate watching Cassie and Molly and Sophia walk down the road, chatting away while I wait with Sam for someone to pick us up. Sam is fine about it all. He likes the new house. He doesn't care about the peeling wallpaper and the stained carpets. He loves the garden. It's wild and rough and that's heaven to Sam.

The worst part of all is watching the new Year 3 girl, Jasmine, walk home with her mum. They always wave at me as if we are friends. They bought our old house. Jasmine probably puts her bag on the lovely white banister and goes and lies down on her bed and looks at the clouds on the ceiling. My clouds. Mine.

Mum pulls up and we both get in. "Good day?" she says. I don't say anything. I don't want to talk. Sam starts rambling on about some bird called a nuthatch that he saw at lunchtime.

"Are you absolutely sure it wasn't a butpatch?" says Mum, elbowing me gently as she waits for us to put our seat belts on. "Or a wutmatch." My mouth is desperate to smile but I bend my lips so it can't. I slump down and stare at the parade of kids passing by.

Mum restarts the engine. Sam rummages in his bag and gets out his magazine. I think of the list again and I feel a bit sick and cross. All mixed up. When I get like this it's like little insects are chasing around inside me. A kid at school had scabies once. It's this thing where little mites live under your skin and make you itch and itch. That's how I feel right now. Like thousands of little mites have tunnelled under my skin.

"You haven't returned the uniform order letter for Valley High," I say, my words all snappy and sharp. "Sophia said the deadline is this week. Everyone else has sent it in."

Mum pulls away. "Um," she says. "No, I haven't yet. I'll get that sorted."

I stare out of my window, trace a line of bird mess that's been there for weeks.

"And there was a list. Of people going to the Year Seven welcome day. And I'm not on it."

Mum's phone rings through the speakers.

"Sorry," she says. "I'll have to take this quickly."

"Course you do," I snap. Mum answers it and her boss's voice booms through the car. It's funny how she tells us she never likes to talk while driving, even though she's hands-free. Funny how right now, when I've put her on the spot, funny how *now* she's talking. Surinder starts rambling on about tests and the clinic and trials and Mum answers her with boring science stuff and they talk all the way home. And then I feel a bit bad because Surinder says that things need to be looked at 'more carefully' and Mum sighs a bit and grips the steering wheel. Mum's job at the laboratory sounds super hard. But she had to take it. She had to earn more money. After Dad's accident, there were lots of things that 'had' to happen.

She parks the car and they are still talking. Sam jumps out, flings his bag at the front door and then races round the side to the garden. I'm going to wait. She's going to answer me. But she just puts her boss on to her mobile and climbs out and keeps talking.

One great, big *sarcoptes scabiei* races through me. That's what one mite is called. I memorized it. I never even knew the poor kid in Year 3 who had them. But Cassie made up some stupid story that we had been spotted buying ice cream together and I had scabies too. I get eczema sometimes on my wrists, little sore patches that need cream.

She pointed at the tiny red spots and told everyone I had the dreaded mites. She went on and on about it, as if it was the funniest joke ever. So I learned everything I could about scabies and by the time everyone had forgotten about it, I was convinced I *did* have them. Mum found me crying one day, really crying. She sat on the bathroom floor next to me and waited and hugged me and I told her. We went straight to the pharmacy. The lady was really nice and said it was perfectly normal to worry about such things. She took me and Mum into a quiet room and asked me some questions and said she was certain I didn't have them. Mum bought me a chocolate bar, a huge one with biscuit chunks, and I felt so much better.

Mum knocks on the window, the phone still glued to her ear and signals at me to get out. I shake my head. No time for Mum now to sit next to me and hug me and wait for me to talk. Oh no. I slide down further in my seat and look away. She goes inside the house, still talking and I just sit there for a while, staring at the front door and the peeling paint and the piles of bricks. They've been sat there for months. Dad was going to build a bit of wall at the front of the drive. But then his leg was bad again and he never got going. Sam has made them into a bug hotel. Spider webs link up across the top bricks.

It starts to get hot in the car so I open the door and let the cool breeze blow in.

Molly wanted to ask Miss Riley about the list. She wanted to see my name on it. There, in black and white. But I didn't want to ask. Because I have a very strong feeling that my name wasn't on the list. And then Cassie would be right, which always makes her smile in that annoying 'told you so' way.

No one comes back out to get me. I slump down further in my seat and then I hear the school bus from Thornberry, the high school on this side of town, trundle by. It stops just along the road. I stare in the wing mirror and watch and wait for the kids to pass by our house. They all seem very tall. The uniform is green. Who wears a green uniform? And the girls have pleated skirts. Apparently, the pleats make it hard to hitch the skirts up. I heard about that in October, when we went to the school open evening. I walked round chewing gum, refusing to take part, telling anyone who asked that I was going to Valley High. Mum and Dad were so cross. I only know about the skirt because while I was having a pee, I heard two girls talking. They were washing their hands and I caught bits when the water stopped. They were moaning about the new skirts and how they couldn't roll the waistband over.

It was horrid, that trip. I was so mad, so determined not to take part. And then it got worse. Mum was upset with me and asked Dad to drive home. But his leg was too stiff to drive so Mum had to, both hands gripping the steering wheel except when she had to lift one to quickly wipe her eyes with a crumpled tissue. Dad sat very still, breathing hard, and I slumped down in the back seat, staring out of the window.

Dad's accident changed everything. He had been away, helping his friend build a house and he had left late to get home. He had driven too fast over a patch of ice. His own fault. That's what he says. Spun the car and banged one side of it into a tree. The phone call had been late at night. Gran and Pops were staying, helping Mum while Dad had been away. They could still do that then. Pops could cope then. The phone rang and rang and when Mum answered it, she screeched a little and shouted for Gran and I knew something bad had happened to Dad. I lay very still, trying to make out the shapes of my clouds on the ceiling, trying to trace the outline in the dark and hoping that if I could make the whole cloud join up, everything would be OK.

It took a long time for him to get better. Months in hospital, months in a wheelchair. He couldn't build houses. We weren't sure if he would *ever* be able to build houses again. We didn't have much money. We had to sell our lovely house and buy a cheaper one, out of town. And that's how we ended up here.

There is a tap on the window. Dad is there, holding Sam's bag and a glass of juice.

"Come on," he says. "Bad day?" I peel myself out of the car and take the juice and lean in to him. He smells good. He strokes my hair. We stand for a second and then I hear voices and another group of high schoolers tumble by, yelling and tugging at each other and I quickly break away from Dad and turn back to get my bag. I unzip it and stuff my jumper inside and zip it back tight. I check the kids have passed and then I look at Dad.

"I haven't got a place at Valley High, have I?"

Dad pulls his hand through his hair. He moves from one foot to the other. And then he looks at me and his eyes are watery, like they were for so long last year.

"No, Amy love." He sniffs hard and rests his hands on my shoulders. "We've tried everything. We are *trying* everything, but I'm sorry, right now, you're down for Thornberry." And then he hugs me hard and I stare at the pile of bricks and a spider on its web, scuttling along one of the threads. "I do have some good news, though," says Dad, one arm wrapped around me as he leads me round the back of the house. "I've been signed fit for work. I heard today." He smiles, really smiles and that makes my heart jump because since his accident, Dad's smile has never been quite the same. The scar has pulled it slightly to one side and sometimes I still notice, as if the old one is hiding underneath.

"That's great, Dad," I say.

"It means I can agree a date to start taking on some new building projects and I can get going on this pile again." He wipes his hand along the windowsill, pulling at the splintered wood and then looks up at the roof.

"Look, Ames," he says, pointing to the sky. "A dinosaur." I follow his eyes, look up past the roof at the cloud passing by, three white strands pulling out like the horns of a triceratops. It's our thing, looking for shapes in clouds. I try to smile but I can't take part in our cloud game right now.

"I miss the old house," I say, quickly turning away. It will spoil Dad's news if he sees me start to cry. I don't know why I'm crying. I don't know if it's because I'm going to Thornberry or because I miss my old home or because I'm still mad with Mum.

There are so many reasons right now.

Three

"I love him when he's like that." Mum leans against the bathroom door and watches Maxi kicking in his little rubber seat, the water flying everywhere. "He likes it when you bath him." I pick up the sponge and rub Maxi's back. He screeches with joy, pulls at my hair. I don't say anything. "Dad told me you two had a little chat. About schools." I lather up the soap and wash Maxi's feet and toes. He squeals and pulls his legs away. "Amy, did you hear me?"

"I heard you," I say but I say it like she's just told me she's bought new shampoo or dinner's ready. I know I'm being unfair, taking it all out on Mum, but I can't help it. I don't want to talk because I know if we talk, I'll probably just let rip right now. She kneels down next to me and puts Maxi's bath book in his hands. He throws it across the room and it lands in the loo.

"I'm really sorry, love. I know it's not what we planned or what you want but Thornberry is a fantastic school. We'll go for another look round." She smooths my hair, rubs my back, smiles at Maxi. "Things are going to get better. Dad's so excited about working again." I sigh deeply. Clever one, Mum. I can't be annoyed about Dad's news, can I? "We can start doing up this amazing house."

Never mind.

Too much.

Off I go. "*Amazing?!* I *hate* this house. It's old and leaky and cold and it smells and I hate it. I loved the old house. I know we had to move. Had to save money… Blah, blah, blah." Mum takes her hand off my back and reaches for Maxi's towel. I'm really going for it now. It's like I can't stop. "But I hate it, OK? I want to go to Valley High. I don't want to wear a pleated skirt and know no one at all. No one!"

Mum wipes her hands on the towel. I glance at her. Her eyes are wide, lips tight. She leans on the bath to stand up. "You do know one person going to Thornberry," she says. "That nice girl Dana at dance. I overheard her mum talking to Jamila after class last week and she said Dana was going there."

I toss the sponge into the water and stand up and walk out. Maxi screeches loudly. He wants me to come back. But I'm gone, I'm out of there. I charge into my bedroom and slam the door hard. I throw myself on to the bed and yell into my pillows.

It's only then I see Mum has bought me a new top for street dance. It's not the one I wanted. It's the purple one that was in the bargain bucket by the front door of the dance shop. She's folded it really neatly and left a note that has a whole line of kisses on it.

Four

"Are you excited to dance today?" asks Gran, twisting round from the front of the car to look at me.

"Yeah," I say. "Can't wait."

We pass the big supermarket and stop at the lights. I bend down to get my bag ready.

"She's always excited to dance, hey, love?" Mum tries to catch my eye. We had a quick hug this morning but we haven't really been OK since yesterday.

"That's good," says Gran. "Your mum said there's a girl there who's going to Thornberry. How lovely!"

I glance up at the back of Mum's head, pull my lips tight, narrow my eyes. I don't say anything, just mumble about my things not fitting in my bag.

"We're going to do a bit of shopping while you're in class, Amy," says Mum, driving round the back of the shops to the dance studio. She's changing the subject, moving it away from Thornberry and Dana. "Pops needs some new slippers."

"And pyjamas," says Gran.

"Why didn't he come with you?" I ask.

Gran sighs. "He's finding it hard to be away from home at the moment." She spins round to look at me. "And he wanted to finish a TV programme he was watching about leopards." I'm not sure I believe Gran. I think she said that so I don't worry. But it's a bit late for that. We all worry about Pops right now.

We pull up at the dance studio and Mum finds a parking space.

"He's finding it hard enough to be *at* home," says Mum, "let alone away from it," and she squeezes Gran's hand. I'm glad Mum hasn't tried to make me think he's watching leopards.

"Poor Pops," I say.

Mum turns the engine off and we sit in silence. "I'm phoning him every hour today," she says, holding up her phone.

I lean forward and kiss Gran on the cheek. And then I kiss Mum.

"Thanks for the top," I say and she smiles. "See you in a bit."

Gran reaches back with her hand and taps my knee. And then she sits up and moves her arms up and down and points her leg straight.

"Do a windmill move for me!" she says. "The one you showed us last week!"

"You mean a helicopter, Gran!" I laugh and she nods.

"I've been practising!" she says. "Pops and I are hoping to sign up soon!"

* * *

Dana stares at my new dance top. She stares at it as if it's got flashing lights. She pulls at her hair and lifts one corner of her mouth, just ever so slightly. She does this a lot and I can never tell if it's a smile or a smirk. Dana has this way of making me feel as if I shouldn't be here. And I don't know why.

"In line, please," calls Jamila. "Let's get warmed up," and we all take our places. I start to feel the rhythm, loosen up. We move on to shuffles and tic-tac-toe and link up the moves. I stare at the mirror and follow Jamila's lead. We all do. Dana misses the beat and stops and tries again but she can't pick it up. She glares at herself in the mirror and then she glances at Sophia and me and the others, as if she's trying to work out who knows she can't get it.

"Quick break," calls Jamila. We stop to get a drink. Dana's bottle is next to mine. We both glug and I look for Sophia but she has gone to the loo.

Jamila is finding new music, scrolling through her phone. Dana shoves her bottle under her arm, picks at her nails. I feel like I should say something but I don't know what, so I put my drink down and stretch.

"New top?" says Dana. She keeps picking her nails. I don't want to answer. I bend over, touch my toes, rub my hands up and down my hamstring. "Where did you get it?" she asks. I glance at her. Her hair falls in two straight curtains, either side of her face. She does this, Dana. Asks something really normal but it never feels like you're having a normal chat. It makes my mouth feels like it's lined with the gooey cement Dad uses. All sticky so I can't get the words out.

"Was it from the dance shop?" she says.

Jamila claps her hands.

"I think so," I mumble and I move over to take my spot.

Sophia dashes in from the loo and joins me, hitching her hair back up and giggling about some joke scribbled on the loo wall. I feel better with her by my side.

"Amy," says Jamila, waving at me to join her. "Come forward. We're going to go over the routine and you had it perfect last week." I wince a little. I don't like being at the front, everyone watching me.

"Did I?" I mutter.

"And Dana," says Jamila. "Keep an eye on Amy and follow her lead." Dana blinks hard and picks at her nails again, as if she's not really paying attention.

I take a few steps. The music starts. I link the moves and tag on the backspin. I look in the mirror. Sophia is flying, her body flowing with the moves. Dana has lost the routine already, her nose wrinkled in the way it does when she can't keep up.

Dana is the only person I know going to Thornberry. I think about that and for a moment I forget that the helicopter comes next but I save it and close my eyes and just let the dance run through me. One spin, then another and then I giggle a little to myself as I imagine Gran and Pops joining in, Pops' battered tartan slippers flashing through the helicopter move.

Five

Mr Hibbert takes the register. He adds our three names on at the end. We are sitting at the back in a huddle on the chairs that we carried through from Year 6. There might as well be one of those giant arrows hanging over our heads with a sign saying 'Odd ones out'.

"So," says Mr Hibbert. "We have Amy, Ralph and Jay joining us for the day."

"Why?" shouts Sanjit.

"Because," says Mr Hibbert, "all the other Year Six children are at Valley High today."

"Where are *they* going then?" says Sanjit, pointing at us. A lot of the Year 5 kids have twisted in their chairs to look round.

"Other great schools," says Mr Hibbert. He sounds just like my parents.

"I'm going to the City Drama School," says Ralph. "It's an acting academy. I'm going to study speech and drama."

Course you are, Ralph. The whole of Year 6 knows all about you and your speech and drama. "I had to have two auditions and an interview…" He offers to perform a poem from his audition.

I stare out of the window. This is bad enough without sitting here listening to Ralph. Jay says nothing either. He shifts in his seat and stares at the desk, arms folded. He only came to our school in Year 4 and he's in the other Year 6 class so I don't really know him. He plays football on the county squad with Cassie's brother Josh. And he sometimes stands near me and Sam after school, waiting to get picked up. His dad comes in a really flash car that rumbles. That's all I know.

Ralph is still going. Mr Hibbert can't shut him up. He glances at his watch.

"Last line, I think, Ralph," he says. "We really do need to move on."

The class start work. Mr Hibbert joins us at the back and passes out our maths books with some exercises that Miss Riley and the other Year 6 teacher have set us.

"Does it make sense?" he asks. We nod and open up the books. Ralph just doodles down the side, smiling to himself, his mouth still reciting the poem. I get out my pencil case. Jay looks over at Mr Hibbert and then he looks across the desk and behind him. The tables are clear. He has nothing with him.

"Want to borrow a pencil?" I ask. He goes to say something but then he just nods and takes the one I'm holding out and starts his work.

◆ ◆ ◆

The PE shed reminds me of the garage at our new house. It's full of cobwebs and dirt and it smells.

"If you can just empty the whole thing," says Mr Hibbert, "and lay everything out on the grass, that would be such a help. I need to sort out equipment to take to the District Sports event tomorrow and get the hut tidied up for September."

"Do we get paid?" asks Ralph. Mr Hibbert stares at him.

"I thought you'd prefer to do this, Ralph, but you are very welcome to join the class inside," says Mr Hibbert. "We're going over the end of year test this afternoon."

Ralph shakes his head.

Mr Hibbert gives us instructions and then goes back into the classroom.

Ralph grabs the tub of tennis rackets. Jay reaches for a football and kicks it in the air.

"What school are you going to?" I ask him, reaching for a box of plastic cones.

He stares at me for a second, kicks the ball again, looks away. I don't think Jay wants to talk. But then he says, "Thornberry."

"Oh, me too," I say. "At the moment. I still want to go to Valley High. I'm eighth on the waiting list."

He nods and takes the ball outside, dragging a box of foam javelins with him.

"Did you say you're going to Thornberry?" says Ralph. I nod and he makes a face as if I've just said I'm going to the school of pain and vomit. And then it's quite funny because I look at Jay and he makes the same face behind Ralph's back but he does it like he's a famous actor on the stage, one arm in the air, just like Ralph had done when he performed the poem. I have to bend down and rummage in the box of cones so Ralph doesn't see me laughing.

Six

There are hundreds of Year 6 kids in different-coloured tops. We have found the best shady spot on the field, tucked under a little tree. The loudspeaker bellows out:

"It's a hot day this year at District Sports! Keep drinking water, folks – lots of it!"

The last hurdles racers fly past us.

"Why would anyone choose to do that?" says Molly, wincing as one lad clips the top of the bar.

"Ooh, there's Zoe and Sahira from Valley High," says Cassie, waving madly across the field. "They can't see us!" She grabs me with one hand as if it's important I don't walk away, that I stay to see this. "They were the *funnest* girls you can imagine. Zoe has amazing nails and these beads in her hair. So cool. I'm going to meet up with them over the summer." She shouts across the field, "Zoe! Sahira! Over here!" The girls look over and smile and wave. Cassie lets go of me and waves back frantically and sighs as if they are her new BFFs. Then she jumps up and checks no one is on the track and runs over to speak to them, tapping the hurdles as she goes, stopping to jump over one to make them laugh. It does make them laugh but only because she misses the top and ends up falling flat on her face.

"She doesn't really know them," says Molly, leaning against the tree. "We just spoke to them for a bit in the free time."

"Oh," I say, feeling a little relieved. "Are they in your form?"

Molly nods and hugs her knees.

I start to say, '*Maybe they can be the new triple besties,*' but it sounds a bit mean, so I don't.

We sit and watch as the next race lines up. The loudspeaker bellows to keep the track clear and Cassie jumps up and down and grabs the girl with beads and shrieks a bit, as if she's going to be trapped on their side for the whole afternoon. I wave my hand, beckoning her back over but part of me wants her to stay there with her new best friends and just leave me with Molly.

I often feel that way with Cassie. But we always end up back together, the three of us re-forming like three parts of a triangle, just like it's been since Reception.

The whistle blows. It's the 400-metre final. One lap of the track. Cassie's brother Josh darts out in front.

Sophia joins us and we link arms and yell for the Ashleigh students. There are ten different primary schools and everyone is shouting for their runners.

When they've passed us, Cassie jogs back across the track.

"Do you want to meet the girls?" she says to me. She is hot, her fringe stuck to her forehead with sweat.

I shake my head, keep watching the race.

"Why not?" she asks, wiping her hair back.

We clap and yell at them to go faster.

"I want you to meet them," says Cassie, digging her elbow into my side.

"Josh is winning!" I say, pointing at the other side of the track. "Look – they're almost at the finish line!" Cassie glances over to watch her brother but Jay passes Josh at the last moment and wins the race. Everyone cheers and shouts, all around the field.

The loudspeaker bellows out: "First place, Jay Parker, Ashleigh Primary, with Josh Bennett a close second and Elijah Simms from Selby Primary in third."

Cassie scoffs a little. "They should really say J-J-Jay Parker."

I stare at her. I don't know what she means.

"Sometimes," says Sophia, glaring at her, "you can be so cruel."

Cassie tuts and looks across the field. "Well, I'll just hang out with my new friends then." She runs back over the track but the girls have gone. She sits down and fiddles with the laces on her trainers, her new Valley High water bottle hanging out of her mouth.

"I'm glad she's on her own," says Sophia.

I don't say anything. I feel sorry for Cassie now. She can be *such* a pain but I see sides of her that the others don't. Like last night. She popped over after the day at Valley High. I thought she'd just come to show off her plastic-covered planner and school bottle but she came with a teething ring for Maxi. She loves Maxi. He's been in pain with his teeth and after the open day she had gone to the chemist and bought him this ring you put in the freezer. He chews on it and it really helped last night.

The loudspeaker bellows across the field again: "Next race. All Year Six girls, get ready, please!"

I call Cassie's name and wave at her to come back. She turns her head away, stares down the track pretending not to have heard.

"Just leave her," says Sophia behind me. "I bet you can't wait to go to Thornberry and not have her following you all the time."

I spin round to look at Sophia but she is bent over now, touching her toes, rubbing the back of her legs.

I don't know what to say. She comes upright again, tosses her hair over her shoulder and jogs away.

The loudspeaker blares. "Year Six girls' 100 metres. Everyone's running this one! Come on down, Year Six girls."

"Oooh, that's us," says Molly. She shoves her plait in her mouth, the end sticking out like a rope. "I suppose we have to do this."

"Yep," I say. "It'll be fine." We walk down to the start line. It's hot and sticky standing out in the open. I look back over my shoulder. Cassie is watching us but she looks away and walks down the track by herself.

I think about what Sophia said. I've never thought of Cassie as following me. She's just always there.

"I know she's being a pain," says Molly. "But she's really worried, you know, about not having you with us." I nod and we gather at the back for our heat. "We all are," says Molly, patting her thighs as if they need to be told how to run. "I bet you're whizzing up the waiting list, though."

I shrug. "Doubt it. Who's going to drop out now?"

"My dad said people move house," says Molly.

"Yep," I say and I think of *my* old house and my tummy feels a bit odd.

The announcer calls out the first heat. I look around me, wonder which girls are going to Thornberry. And then I see

Dana. She has a Selby Primary top on. She catches my eye but then she quickly looks away.

We line up. Molly is in the race before mine. She looks back at me and makes her knees wobble like jelly, which makes us both laugh. She bends down to stretch and while she's upside down the whistle blows and I have to bite my giggles as Molly whips back up and starts five paces behind everyone else.

"Go for it, Moll!" I yell and then I line up for my own race. Dana is in the next lane. Just my luck. We set off and our arms get a bit tangled so I whip mine back and move to the side.

The race is over in a flash. We gather at the end, panting and laughing.

"I absolutely hated it," says Molly.

"I loved it," says Sophia, smoothing the 'First' sticker on her jumper.

Cassie comes over with a girl I haven't seen before. She is happy again, the sulky face wiped clean.

"Amy, this is Rosie. We were in the same hundred-metre heat and she's going to Thornberry and I said how you are *very* lonely right now and don't know *anyone* and would Rosie meet you?"

I stare at Cassie.

I can't believe she's doing this.

"She's not lonely, Cass," says Molly, glaring at her.

"Hi," says Rosie.

"Hi," I say, picking at my 'Well done' sticker. Cassie stares at us, one to the other. She's enjoying this. It's all a bit icky so I say, "What school do you go to?"

"Kingsway Primary," says Rosie.

"Cool," I say.

Rosie starts telling me about her school and how everyone is going to Thornberry. "I've never heard of someone going who knows *no one*," she says, her eyes super wide. "That must be really hard."

I shrug. "I know two people."

"Oh," says Rosie. "Well, that's OK."

I nod. I can hardly say, *Yes, one girl who doesn't like me and a boy I don't know at all.*

"Do you like the pleated skirt?" Rosie asks. I shake my head. "Have you ordered yours yet?" I shake my head again. "I heard they've sold out," she says.

"You have to wear a *pleated* skirt?" says Cassie. "OMG, I feel *so* sorry for you." Rosie stares at her as if she's just made it a hundred times worse.

I look round for Molly or Sophia but they've moved away. They're standing with the two girls from Valley High that Cassie was with earlier. Molly is laughing and Sophia is pointing across the field, showing them something.

Rosie taps me on the arm. I turn back. Her eyes are so wide it looks like her pupils are going to pop out.

"You really ought to order a skirt, you know, in case there are none left."

I don't want to talk about this any more so I quickly mutter, "I need the loo," and turn away. The portable toilets are on the edge of the field, past the announcing desk and the prize table. There's a big sign that says 'Winning medals here'. A few kids are waiting in line. I run towards it, aiming for the loos behind.

I will be the only Year 7 girl in the wrong skirt.

I won't know anyone.

Dana will tell her friends to ignore me.

My throat tightens and dries and a pain aches in my tummy so I stop and walk a bit and try very hard not to cry. And then I see Jay. He's in the medal line. He looks over. I wipe my eyes and then brush my hands down my T-shirt, as if I've wiped off grass or dust from my face. He points at me, at the ground. I stop walking. He jogs over and picks something up and passes it to me. It's a 'Well done' sticker.

"I-it's yours," he says. I look down at my top and see mine is missing.

"Oh," I say. "Thanks." I stick it back on my top, try and smooth the edges. Try again while I blink back the tears. It won't stick any more, so I stuff it in my pocket. I look up.

"They don't last long," says Jay. "The stickers, I mean."

"Doesn't matter too much for sixth place!" I say. He smiles. "You've done really well," I say, pointing at the medal around his neck and his two first stickers stuck to his T-shirt. "Are you waiting for your other medal?"

He nods, twists his medal, looks at the picture of the runner on the front. "I-I wouldn't get one in maths," he says. "Or English."

"Me neither," I say. "Bet Ralph has loads for drama." He smiles again. He goes to say something but then he stops, fiddles with his medal. Tries again. Eventually he just raises one hand as a goodbye and runs back to the line.

I go over to the portaloos. I think of Ralph, getting his drama medal, standing on the podium performing his favourite part. It makes me smile. I open the door and go inside and wait for a bit, just long enough that anyone watching would think I'd had a quick pee and then I open the door and jump back out and breathe the fresh air and I feel better.

Molly runs over.

"You OK?" she says.

"Yep." We walk back across the field. The wind picks up, blowing our ponytails over our shoulders.

"Just ignore Cassie. She's being stupid."

I nod. For a moment I can't remember why Cassie had upset me but then I see Rosie by the water table and it comes back. She sees me and waves and I wonder if Cassie was just trying to do a nice thing, asking Rosie to meet me. You never quite know with Cassie.

The loud speaker calls the girls' 100-metre final.

"Come on," says Molly. "Let's go and yell for Sophia." She takes my arm and we run over to the side of the track. The whistle goes and we shout out her name, so loudly that my ears hurt. The girls fly by, super fast and it's hard to see who wins. I watch all the runners at the end, all the different tops and colours and schools. I can pick out the Ashleigh runners, like you pick out your family in a crowd and it makes me think that I won't have this any more. There will be no friendly faces. I will be alone.

Molly grabs me. "Sophia won! Let's go and see her!" and we run together, down the side of the track and I let the warm breeze catch my face and just try to think about the summer holidays coming up and how I'll see my friends all the time and that September is ages and ages away.

Seven

"Was it fun?" says Mum.

"Nope," I say.

"Did you meet anyone new?"

"No."

I stare out of the window, watch the kids walk by, heading for the car park. Jay runs past, his medals clinking around his neck, ear pods in.

"I just thought maybe," says Mum, turning down the radio, "with all those schools there, you might have met someone going to Thornberry."

My little scabies friends wake up, trickling through me. I pull out my hair band, twist it around my finger. "Yes, Mum, I met five new girls in the hurdle race who are all going to Thornberry and they were so nice I'm going to ditch all my old friends and be happy forever."

"Well, that's good," says Mum. "It was worth going then."

Oh my God. I hate it when she does that but I still want

to smile so I busy myself with the hair band again, putting my hair back up so I've got something to do.

"I wish you'd have let me or Dad come and watch."

I sink down in my seat. "I jumped into a pit of sand and ran in one race and came sixth."

"Better than last," says Mum.

"Sixth *was* last," I say and I flick my head away quickly because I know we are both smiling. "Sophia won though, so that was good." I'm about to tag on, '*And Jay, who's going to Thornberry,*' but I don't want to.

Mum drives down the road and stops to let kids cross. Maxi gives out a little whimper. He is falling asleep, clutching his giraffe. I turn round and pull his blanket over him.

"Thanks," says Mum.

We're quiet all the way out of the field gates. The wind has really picked up now and the sky has turned dark, low grey clouds gathering in the distance.

"Think it might pour down," says Mum. "Do you want something to eat?"

"Only if it's a burger."

"There's a drive-thru just down here."

"'K."

Mum's phone rings. It's Surinder. Her name comes up on the big, square screen in the car. She ignores it.

"I can't believe it's your last day of primary tomorrow."

I turn away and look out of the window. I'm hot and sweaty and hungry.

"I phoned about the waiting list today," says Mum. "You've whizzed up to seventh."

"Great," I say. "I'm really flying up that list."

We drive past the row of shops and I stare at them, the window displays flashing past.

"I've juggled my day tomorrow," says Mum, "so I can be there with Dad at the final assembly."

"Can Gran have Maxi?" I ask as we pull up at the drive-thru. Mum lets me order the deluxe and an extra large milkshake with all the toppings. We move to the collection window. "I don't want him screeching through it," I say. "Like at Christmas."

Mum looks at Maxi in the mirror.

"What, that angel in his Father Christmas suit?"

"Yeah, that angel who screeched so loud that Balthazar had to wait a whole minute to pass over his myrrh and then he forgot his lines."

"Oh, I think it enhanced the performance," says Mum.

We pull into a bay and Mum passes me the burger. I unwrap it and take a massive bite. The hot sauce oozes. It's so good. There's a flash of lightning and then a rumble of thunder.

Mum reaches out and strokes my hair. "I need to talk to you about the next few weeks."

I pause mid-bite. Something makes me feel uneasy. But I bite down and grunt that I'm listening.

"Gran's had a fall."

I spin round to look at Mum. Sauce runs down my chin.

"She's fine! But she's hurt her ankle. She's had it checked out and it's badly sprained. She's limping around and needs help. We'll have to step in."

I wipe my chin, chew slowly, pick at the bread roll, pulling crumbs away.

"Step in?" she says, nudging me. "Get it? Bad ankle ... we 'step' in. I'm so funny."

This doesn't feel funny. A few big, fat raindrops land on the window.

"Why don't they come and stay with us?" I ask.

"Well, that might be possible when the house is done but not right now. Also, Pops is finding it harder and harder to be away from his routine and he's getting a bit –" she sits up and tightens her grip on the steering wheel – "worse."

"How?"

"When I took Gran shopping the other day, he cooked sausages in the oven."

"What's wrong with that?"

"They were still in their packaging."

"Oh."

"The kitchen was filled with smoke and the plastic had melted to the oven shelf. If Gran had been any longer, it could have been horrendous."

"Oh."

"So here's the plan," says Mum. "You, me, Maxi and Sam are going to move in with Gran and Pops on Saturday." She's speeding up, the words flying out before I can stop her. "We can't leave them alone so coming and going will be hard. Dad is going to stay at home, and Uncle Jack is coming over with his mates Filip and Brian and they're going to use the time to start working on the house. They've been so kind and put other jobs on hold." She sniffs hard then takes a quick breath. "Filip, bless him, put the word out, about Dad's accident and how hard things have been. So many mates have offered to help. The plan is to replaster, lay new carpets, rip out the kitchen. Really get going on making it a lovely home for us all."

She starts the car, puts on the windscreen wipers to clear the rain. It's bouncing off the bonnet and pouring on to the windows.

We drive out of the shopping area and back on to the main road.

I slurp my milkshake. I'm relieved it's only Gran's ankle but I start to think of all the things coming up in the next few weeks, the last few weeks I'm truly going to be with my friends. "How long are we staying?"

Mum stops at the traffic lights, yanks the handbrake on, flicks the windscreen wipers to their fastest speed. I slurp even harder.

"How long?" I say again.

"Two weeks."

"Two weeks!" I yell, spitting cream into the air. "That's not happening."

Cinema trip, last dance session, Cassie's sleepover, Molly's party. There's so much happening in the next two weeks.

"You haven't got a choice on this one, Amy. I'm sorry." The lights change and she pulls away. The road is soaking wet now, the tyres of the cars throwing up spray.

"I don't have a choice on anything at the moment. Where we live. Where I go to school. What I can do in the holidays." I slam the cup down into the holder. Cream sprays on the gear stick. "I'll stay with Dad."

"Not possible. There won't be any water or electrics. Dad's going to stay with Brian. You have to come with me. I've taken most of the time as holiday, so I won't have to go to work."

"I'm not missing Cassie's sleepover on Wednesday or Molly's party. That's in two weeks' time."

"You'll make the party," says Mum. "I promise. But I need you to help me out a bit with the rest."

I slump down.

They promised I could go to Valley High. And that's not happening.

My scabies stir.

The phone rings again. It's Gran.

"Hi," she says when Mum answers. "Just to let you know your dad put the landline phone in the toilet. So it's not working. Call me on my mobile if you need me." Her voice sounds weak, a bit shaky. "And he forgot the neighbour's name today. Paul. Went completely blank."

"OK," says Mum. "Well, we all do that."

"Not when Paul had *just* said his name, twice, ten seconds before."

I glance at Mum. I can't think what to say. And I feel a bit bad now, for going on about the sleepover.

There is a loud crash in the background.

"Better go," says Gran.

We say bye and Gran hangs up.

"She's hopeless with that mobile," says Mum.

Surinder calls again.

"Do you need to take that?" I ask. She shakes her head and presses decline.

"I'll call her back," she says.

"I wish Pops didn't have it," I say. "The memory thing."

"I know," says Mum.

"It's getting really bad, isn't it?" It makes me feel tearful just saying the words.

"Yes, I'm afraid so," says Mum. "But there's lots we can do to help him and he's on the right medication now."

"It's scary," I say.

She turns briefly to look at me.

"It can be," says Mum. "But I don't think Pops sees it that way. We just have to have lots of fun while we can."

I reach for her hand and hold it tight and we stay like that until the next set of lights when she has to let go.

Eight

I can hear Maxi. He's three rows behind. Mum promised she'd get him to sleep but he's loud and shouty. My final day in primary school, my last assembly and all I can think about is Maxi, babbling out across the room.

"Your brother is *so* cute," whispers Sophia, glancing back over her shoulder.

The other Year 6 class are saying their 'golden moments'. I glance down at mine, written on a card on my lap.

> *The time me and Molly and Cassie won the poster competition about reducing food waste and we had a meal out at the pizza place as a prize and the waiters sang to us in Italian and gave us free ice cream.*

It sounds silly now, the bit about the waiters singing. I'm not sure I want to do this. Not in front of everyone. I look up and down the row. Everyone is very still, facing the other class, listening. Cassie is leaning back, legs outstretched, arms folded as if she's a bit bored.

"*The residential trip when Ralph fell in the river...*"

"*The time in Year Five when Mr Hibbert hit the rounders ball and it went over the wall and smashed the neighbour's greenhouse...*"

"*The nativity play in Year Two when I was a camel and the hump fell off...*"

Josh stands up next. His cheeks turn bright red, really quickly, like they do on cartoons. He unfolds his piece of card and shifts from one foot to the other. It's hard to believe Josh and Cassie are twins sometimes. I don't think I've ever seen Cassie nervous.

"The summer school fair when we had the bush tucker trial and I had baked beans tipped over my head."

"Wish I could do that to him every day," mutters Cassie, elbowing me gently. It makes me smile. And then Cassie sighs a bit, leans in to me and whispers, "Oh, here we go. How long have we got?"

Jay stands up. He's the last to read. He taps his card. He goes to speak. But nothing comes. He tries to smile and shifts from side to side. Flicks his fringe a bit. I'm staring at him. I've seen that look before, when I asked him what school he was going to and at the District Sports event. Maxi screeches from the row behind. Everyone laughs a bit. Jay looks up. And then he says, "Football. The time we won the schools' county match and Josh did a brilliant save in the last five minutes and then I-I scored and we all went mad." He sits straight down. Josh grabs him and hugs him and they're laughing and remembering. Everyone claps and cheers. A man standing at the side does a loud whistle sound. I look round. I think it's Jay's dad. He's giving Jay the thumbs up.

I turn to Molly and whisper low. "It must be so hard, when he can't get the words out."

"Yep," she says, clapping hard. "But he did it!"

I turn and look at Cassie. She's picking at her nails, chipping at the little flecks of red polish. I want to say something. I want to tell her that I hate it when she's unkind. I want to take her name off my special memory card. But then the head teacher calls our class forward and we all walk over to the chairs in front and turn to face the crowd. We sit down. Everything is quiet. And then there is a very loud screech. Maxi has seen me. He yells out a load of nonsense and then his toy giraffe sails across the room and bounces off Miss Riley's shoulder.

♣ ♣ ♣

The party food is finished, presents given out, certificates done. Mum is rocking Maxi in the stroller, his little legs sticking out, kicking. We are all outside on the field, the parents and teachers versus kids rounders game well under way.

We cheer as Dad takes up the bat. All my class know how long Dad was poorly for, how long it was until he could walk again. It feels incredible, sitting here in the sunshine, watching Dad in his shorts, the long scar running down his leg.

Jess bowls. Dad takes a huge swing and whacks it. Ralph runs under it, watches it sail in the air.

"That's me out first bat!" laughs Dad, but Ralph stumbles and the ball rolls off his hand and falls to the ground.

"Run!" yells Miss Riley.

We all yell and cheer as Dad runs to first base, second base. Jay is on third and he stumps the base so Dad has to stop.

"Third base!" shouts Dad. "I'll take it!" We all cheer, every one of us.

Cassie's dad, Gareth, steps up next. He's wearing all sporty gear, his baseball cap on back to front. Cassie squirms and pretends to look embarrassed but I think she loves it really, that her dad is super active. He hits the ball and it flies over the field and rolls down into the playground. He sets off, racing around the pitch, catching up with Dad as he jogs past fourth base.

The ball is lost behind the bins. Mr Hibbert starts shifting things to find it.

"Water break!" shouts Miss Riley. "And then we'll swap fielders. Come on, you lot!" she says, waving at us. "Your turn when the ball is found!"

Sophia grunts. "I hate fielding," she says.

Molly picks a few daisies and starts stringing them into a chain. "This is the last time we'll do this," she says. "We've always made daisy chains in the summer, on the field."

"Bring it on," says Sophia. She lies back on the grass, puts one hand over her face to shade her eyes. "I'm so done with it all."

No one says anything.

"Not you guys, of course," she says. "I just can't wait to get to high school. Wear the uniform and take the bus and have a choice at lunch. You know, all that stuff."

"I know *exactly* what you mean," says Cassie.

Molly looks at me and raises her eyebrows and I smile and lean in to her. Cassie was crying an hour ago, floods of tears over her strawberry ice cream, gulping back deep waves of misery, saying that leaving primary was the hardest moment of her life.

I stare across the field, back at our classroom. I can see Mrs Khan, the classroom assistant, taking down all the final display things in the room. Our time here is done. I want to be like everyone else. They know exactly where they're going, who's in their form, where the bus stops. I don't know a thing.

Miss Riley calls us over again.

Sophia jumps up and yells at her mum who is taking the batting spot.

"Go for it, Mum! Whack it hard. I'll bowl." She runs over to take the ball but Jess won't give it up.

"Typical," says Cassie. "Of *course* Jess has to bowl the whole time." She scowls at her. Things are not good between Jess and Cassie. They never are.

"Well," says Cassie. "At least the two of you will be at mine on Wednesday. And the cinema this weekend. We have loads to look forward to."

My mouth goes dry and I pick at the grass next to me. I'm going to miss everything.

"We need to join in," I say and I stand up.

"Let's just go at the back," says Molly, "past third base," and we aim for that part of the field.

"Can you both come early on Wednesday?" says Cassie. "We could go to the park or the pool or something? What do you think? And Mum's going to pre-book the cinema for Sunday so we need to decide what time we want to go. And which movie. There's that sequel on about the dance school in New York."

"Yeah, let's see that one," says Molly. "What do you think, Ames?"

Ralph's granddad puts his stick down and takes the bat and walks up to the box. Miss Riley gives Jess a 'go easy' sign with the bowling.

Cassie stares at me. "Come on," she says. "Which movie?"

"Do we have to decide right now?" I ask.

"I thought you wanted to come. Honestly, I try to arrange these things…"

"I can't make it," I say. They both look at me.

"No ball!" yells Miss Riley. She glares at Jess. "I said *slowly*, Jess!"

"Why?" says Cassie. "That's crazy. It's the holidays."

"I have to go to my gran's house."

"But you said you'd be there," says Cassie and she stomps off and almost walks into Ralph's granddad as he jogs from first to second base.

"I want to be," I mutter. "But I can't."

The ball sails towards us. Molly leaps for it but it rolls past her and we both run after it. We start giggling. We can't get hold of it. I pick it up but drop it and it bounces off my knee. Jess races over and grabs it and throws it hard at fourth base. A big debate starts about whether Jay's dad was out or not. Molly and I wander back, waiting for play to restart.

"Will you make my party?" asks Molly, leaning down to pick another daisy.

"Of course!" I say and she jumps up and throws her head back and hugs me.

"I'm *so* relieved!" she says and I smile and hug her back. Over her shoulder I can see Dad stretching his leg, Mum smiling, her hair blowing in the wind, Maxi's legs still kicking in the pushchair, but slowly now, just little flinches, his final attempt to stay awake.

Nine

"Do we really need *all* this food?" My feet are covered in loaves and potatoes and fruit. I move the huge bunch of bananas and stuff it on the pile between the seats. The car is full, stacked right to the top with our bags and the gear we need for Maxi. You'd think we were moving in with Gran and Pops, not just going for a couple of weeks.

"It all helps," says Mum, staring back at the house. "Come on, Sam!" He jogs down the drive, holding a fresh pack of batteries, squeezing past the giant skip that arrived this morning. Uncle Jack has already started throwing things in it. He was here setting up before anyone was awake, his big white van parked across the end of the drive.

"OK, so you're sorted now," says Dad, hugging him tight. "Set that trap cam and let's see what you get!"

"Gran has that woodland behind the house and all that honeysuckle," says Sam. "Dormice love honeysuckle and I know they've been spotted in the area. It may just be amazing."

May just be amazing.

Sometimes I have no idea how he is my brother. Trying to film a dormouse is his big thing right now. Last summer it was a hedgehog. This summer, a dormouse.

He squeezes into the car and Dad taps on the window.

"Right, I'll pop over in the week," he says to Mum. "Drive carefully, OK? Can you actually see out of the back?"

"Yes, just about," says Mum and she starts the engine.

My phone beeps. It's Cassie.

> Are u sure u can't make it to the movie?
> 🍹 We're all set! U me and Moll

I throw my phone, aiming for the inside of my bag. But it hits the dashboard and lands on a punnet of grapes.

"That'll be interesting," says Mum. "If you break your phone."

I slump down into the seat.

"I really don't care," I say. "It's not as if I can arrange my life anyway."

"You're eleven," she says, turning to settle Maxi. "Kids don't arrange so much at eleven. Just enjoy it."

Dad waves madly from the side of the road. We pull away.

"Cassie wants to go to the cinema tomorrow. Me, her and Moll."

Mum grips the steering wheel.

"I've told you, love. I can't get you back for tomorrow."

My scabies wake up. All of them. Racing around.

"Or the sleepover on Wednesday. Or the last dance session on Tuesday. Jamila has this dance-fest thing planned." I pick up my phone from on top of the grapes and stare at the screen.

"I know it's tricky," says Mum. "Dad and I will get you to Molly's party in two weeks' time. But I'm not sure about the rest. It's over an hour's drive and I can't leave Gran and Pops alone right now."

"They could come with us."

"Pops has started opening the car door at traffic lights."

"Oh."

I text Cassie to say I can't make it. She comes straight back with a sad face emoji. And a poo emoji. And says how sorry she is for me that I have to miss everything. And that she'll ask Sophia instead. Course she will.

"*I* can't go to cubs," says Sam. "It's the last one this week and they're going out late to watch the badger setts. With a badger expert."

"That's hardly the same thing," I say, turning round to glare at him. "Badgers aren't going anywhere, are they? There will always be badgers down in that grotty part of the wood for the stupid cubs to go and watch."

Mum puts her hand up and does this quiet screech thing that she does when she's had enough. "It *is* the same thing to Sam. Now stop it, Amy."

I pull my bag out from under the potatoes, yanking it hard. A punnet of blueberries breaks open and spills down the side. Mum sees it but she doesn't say anything. I put in my ear pods and press play and sink down, wiggling the dodgy wire to make the music come, shoving my feet through the shopping.

Ten

"There's my girl!" says Gran, throwing her arms out. Her crutches clatter to the floor. I fall into her arms, and wrap myself around her, careful not to nudge her bad ankle. She always smells the same, Gran. Of toast and soil and soap. "Oh, did you have to bring that one?" she says, laughing at Maxi in Mum's arms.

"'Fraid so," I say, dumping my bag in the hall. "Where's Pops?"

"Front room," says Gran. "He's excited to see you." Sam and I find him. He's dozing in his chair, his newspaper draped across his chest. I kiss him on his cheek. His eyes open. He blinks for a moment and sits up a little.

"Is that my lovely Amy?" he says, reaching for the paper. "I was just catching up with this wretched climate warming thing. You come to see us, love?"

"Just to help Gran," I say.

"She needs it!" he says, smiling. "I'm quite the handful

these days."

He turns his head slightly and watches Sam. He stares hard, as if he's trying to focus. And then he says, "He'll be out soon," and Sam smiles.

Sam loves Gran and Pops' cuckoo clock. He's always trying to work out when the bird will next appear.

Pops sits back and closes his eyes.

There's a new table by his chair. It's white and plastic and on it there are two things. A huge TV remote control with large numbers and buttons. And a clock. A giant clock, the size of a shoe box with different compartments. The time is on a round face but it's also there in digital numbers. The year, the month and date are shining in red. All staring at Pops as if he needs help to pin himself to this day. As if he is holding on to time because it's slipping from him. I don't like the new white table. It looks like it should be in a hospital, not in this room next to their precious things. Books on every surface. Ornaments and animal statues lined up, rammed in, like they always have been, each with a story to tell from their travels. I run my hands over the shelves, touch the velvet lemur's ears, gently lift the lid of the Swiss musical box and turn the key, just a little. It plays a tune, like it always does.

"Swiss Alps," says Pops, his eyes still closed. "Takes me right there with Suzie. 1963."

Mum comes in and kisses Pops on the cheek. "Come and have a drink," she says, resting her arm on my back. I turn to go and right at that moment the cuckoo comes out of the clock and sings.

"Told you," murmurs Pops with a smile, his eyes open now to watch the little bird fly in and out.

"It's my favourite," says Sam.

I tuck Pops' blanket around his legs and then me and Sam join the others in the kitchen. Gran has made fresh lemonade. Sam wolfs his down and runs out to the garden. It tastes so good.

Gran's sitting in her favourite armchair in the corner of the kitchen, her foot up on a stool.

"Is it painful?" I ask.

"No, it's fine, Amy love. I really can cope. Don't know why your mother makes such a fuss."

"We fuss," says Mum, filling a bowl with all the fruit we brought, "because we love you."

"Am I in the sewing room?" I ask. "I'll go and unpack."

"Yes, I'll come up," says Mum. She glances out at the garden. "Sam's putting up the trap cam on the cherry tree."

"There's a surprise," I say. I look out to the garden. The grass is long, the summer breeze blowing the branches of the tree.

"Let's just hope the dormouse population is booming out there," she says. "Come on."

We head up the stairs. Framed photographs follow the line of the banister. Me with no front teeth, Sam at the zoo with the meerkats, Maxi asleep in his cot. Mum and Dad on their wedding day. Gran and Pops on the beach when they were younger. I always touch that photo. The waves look so real. Pops is looking out to sea, his hair whipped by the wind.

The room is tiny. The door bangs on Gran's sewing machine table. The machine is still up, a piece of cloth stuck under the needle, dust gathered around the metal.

"Really?" I say. I haven't slept in here for a while. I'd forgotten how small it is.

"Well, if you want to be on your own, then yes. I've brought some things to put in later, to make it cosy."

"Cosy is the word," I mutter.

"Yes, well," says Mum, "Sam and Maxi are with me which isn't ideal either. The travel cot will hardly fit." She starts to move things around to make extra space.

I walk to the window, which is about three paces away, and look out over the road. A car swings on to the drive opposite. It has really shiny wheels. I've seen a car just like it but I can't think where.

I take out my phone. My last message to Molly hasn't sent. "Has Gran changed her Wi-Fi code?"

"There isn't any Wi-Fi right now. Gran had to take the box out. It was causing a problem."

"*No Wi-Fi?*" I shout it.

Mum raises both hands and tilts her head. "Keep your voice down."

I look down at my phone again, try to resend the message but I have no signal.

Gran calls up the stairs, "Everything OK? Do you have enough space?"

"Don't say anything to Gran, please," says Mum. "About the Wi-Fi or the room being tiny."

"Of course not." I stare at her and blink hard as if to say, '*I'm not stupid.*' "It's just…"

"I know," says Mum. "It's hard. You want to be in touch. I get it."

There is a sudden clatter downstairs as if pots and pans have been dropped. Maxi cries. A voice shouts for help. Mum spins round and thuds back down the stairs.

I slump on to the floor and look around me. I can sit against one wall and stretch my legs out and touch the sewing machine table on the other. There's a chair and a small chest of drawers, with shelves on each side, every surface covered in an antique or photo frame or roll of knitting wool. On the highest shelves are encyclopedias, twenty-six books in all, covered in red leather. When I was little, Pops would reach me one down and I would line up my dolls and pretend to teach them stuff about oceans and animals and flags of the world. Now I'm worried they will fall on me in the middle of the night and crush me and the local newspaper headline will say: GIRL KILLED BY KNOWLEDGE.

The message to Molly still hasn't sent. I press the little red circle and try again but still nothing. I'm so out of the whole friendship thing. For weeks. I'm out of it all. I'm out anyway, for good, off to a school where I have no friends. Not one. It feels like the rope in the sports day tug of war. I'm at one end, pulling hard, tripping over. Everyone else is at the other end, and the rope is old and splitting and frayed and soon I'll trip and be forced to let go and have no link to them at all. I hug my knees and stare up at the books. Try and find the encyclopedia that would include misery or loneliness but then I'm not sure they cover things like that.

Eleven

Mum has made soup. "It's a bit heavy on the lentils," she says. "Sorry."

"It's heavy on everything," says Sam, dumping his spoon in the gloop.

"It's gorgeous," says Gran. "Such a treat to be cooked for. And lentils are so good for you."

"Why doesn't *he* have to eat it?" says Sam, pointing at Maxi, who's in his high chair, eating bits of cheese. "Think I'd rather have the cheese. And I hate cheese."

"You don't hate cheese," says Mum.

"I do."

"Well, next time we order pizza, we'll leave you out."

Pops puts down his spoon. "Disgusting," he says.

We all stop. Sam smiles a bit as if he wants to agree but he can tell no one else finds it funny. Pops has never said anything like that. Ever.

He stares at his bowl. "Disgusting," he says again. "I

want the normal soup."

Gran gets up and hobbles to the fridge and finds a yoghurt. "Here you go, love. Toffee. Your favourite." She pats his shoulder and blinks hard, wiping her eyes. There's a tear, I'm sure. "I'll make soup again soon." She passes him a teaspoon and sits back down.

We all carry on eating the soup.

Pops takes a big mouthful of yoghurt. A dollop drops from the spoon and lands on his jumper but he doesn't notice. Mum picks up a bit of kitchen roll and passes it to him.

"Here you go, Dad," she says. "You spilled a bit." He looks at her and then he looks at his jumper but he doesn't see the stain. He just keeps eating the yoghurt, wiping the pot clean. Mum tidies up Maxi's food on his tray, keeps busy.

"I'm going to do some woodwork in my shed," says Pops. He stands up and scrapes his chair back.

"Is that a good idea?" asks Gran.

"Why ever not?" says Pops. He stares at her as if she's gone mad. "I always do woodwork after lunch."

"Not for a very long time," says Gran but she says it quietly and he doesn't hear.

"I'm taking biscuits with me," says Pops. He opens the cupboard and takes out a packet of cookies.

We all watch Pops walk towards the back door and cross the garden to his shed. It's as if we're waiting for him to change his mind.

"He'll eat the whole pack, bless him," says Gran.

"So would I," says Sam and we all smile.

"He's not been in his shed for ages," says Gran. "Can someone go with him?"

Mum looks over at Maxi. He's rubbing his eyes, lumps of cheese stuck in his hair. "I need to put Maxi down for a sleep. Can you go with Pops, Amy?" She glances at me. We haven't spoken since the Wi-Fi thing upstairs.

"Of course," I say. It's been a tricky lunch and I'm relieved that I can be helpful again.

"I'll come too," says Sam.

We follow Pops to the shed and go inside. It smells of oil and wood and damp. Pops is standing with his hands on his hips, looking around him. He touches his tools, one by one, tapping through the row of chisels, as if he's choosing which one to use. He switches on the light and puts on the radio. Classical music plays faintly. Pops moves to the workbench and picks up a piece of wood, clamps it into the grippy thing and then takes the biggest chisel and starts working on the wood, over and over, humming along to the music. A shaft of sunlight comes through the window, lighting up the dust, the air sprinkled with it.

"I must show you how to do this."

"We'd like that," I say.

"You've shown me already," says Sam. I elbow him and shake my head.

"Have I?" says Pops. He wheels round and looks at Sam. "Well, of course I have, young Sammy. We made that little horse together, didn't we? A while back. You were nifty with the chisel."

Sam smiles and says, "I'm going outside." He opens the door and the breeze drifts in.

Pops stops for a second, runs his hands over the wood and nods, very gently, and starts working again.

"Yes, I must show you how," he says.

Twelve

My room's looking better. The sewing machine has been boxed up and put away. I've cleared some of Gran's clutter. Mum has brought my pink bedding and the camp bed that is really cosy. She's even strung up some fairy lights.

I've had a long hot shower and my hair is in a towel on my head. Gran bought us welcome gifts. Sam got a huge magnifying glass, Maxi a spinning top and I got a pamper pack. I've used the face mask and my skin is feeling super sparkly. I have two big spots right now and I've let them have a true deep airing.

Sam is watching TV downstairs with Maxi. Gran found a bunch of old DVDs. Tom and Jerry screech through the house.

The doorbell rings. I try to see who it is but I can't from my window. There's a little covered porch over the front door so I look down on the tiled roof.

The DVD pauses and Gran calls up the stairs.

"Amy love, could you get it? I'm with the boys and your mum's still with Pops. He won't stop carving. And I've just put ice on my ankle. I'm right here if you need me. It might be a parcel."

I don't want to answer the door. I want to keep sorting my room. But I peel myself up and pad down the stairs.

I open the door.

It's Jay. Jay Parker from Ashleigh.

I stare at him and he stares at me.

"Hi." I smile a bit. The towel feels heavy on my head. "Yes," I say.

Yes? Why did I say yes? What a stupid thing to say.

Jay looks at me a bit funny, his face frozen, as if he's seen a ghost or someone he really wasn't expecting. Which I suppose he has. And then he realizes who I am.

"Oh, hi," he says. "I-I didn't recognize you with the ... y-you know." He lifts his hand and points at my wrapped head and then puts it down quickly as if it was rude.

I pat the towel and then gasp a little as I wonder if he was pointing at my two beacon spots instead. *I didn't recognize you with those two great big flashing splats on your face...*

"Um," says Jay. He looks back over his shoulder, across the road. His dad has parked the car on the drive and is getting out.

"I saw your dad's car from my window upstairs." I point up, as if Jay wouldn't know where an upstairs window is. As I do, my head tips and the towel slips off. I grab it and wrap it round my neck, pulling one hand through my hair that is now like a nest of mangled twigs. "I knew I recognized it. I just couldn't work out where from."

Jay nods and smiles and spins round to look at the car. "You can't miss it really!"

"Just one pint, Jay," shouts his dad, giving Jay the thumbs up, like he did at the assembly on the last day of school. "To see us through. If Susan doesn't mind."

I don't know who Susan is.

"I'm not sure who Susan is," I say.

"Oh," says Jay.

"Who is it?" shouts Gran. "Shall I come?" And then I feel really stupid because I realize *Gran* is Susan.

"Um," I say. "I don't know. Maybe"

Oh my God. *Um, I don't know. Maybe.* I wrap the towel tighter around my neck.

Gran's crutches tap on the wooden floor in the lounge. The door opens and she joins us, calling back to Sam to keep an eye on Maxi. She has an ice pack strapped to her ankle, wrapped in a white cover.

"Hi, Jay, how are you?"

I stare at Gran. It all seems so odd. Gran knows him.

"Um," says Jay. "Yeah, fine thanks." He looks down at the ground and then up again and shifts his feet. And then he looks straight at me and then at Gran, one to the other. I wait for a second. "D-dad was wondering if we could borrow a pint of milk."

"Of course," says Gran. "No worries at all." She hobbles off to the kitchen.

I turn back and look at Jay. I'm not sure what to say. Jay is wearing full football kit with studs on. He's muddy. So I say, "Have you been playing football?" Sometimes my mouth and my brain do not talk to each other. They just work completely on their own.

"Yeah," says Jay.

Sam bursts out of the lounge yelling, "Buzzards, buzzards!" He races to the front door and points up, way high. There are two big birds circling. He races away again, yelling, "Watch Maxi! I'm getting my binoculars."

Maxi crawls over, one hand gripping his spinning top, which bangs along the floor. He stops beside me, sits back and passes it to me, grunts for me to show him how it works. He only has a T-shirt and nappy on and it's full. Super full so that it squidges out around him when he sits. He grunts again. You have to plunge the spinner quite hard several times and he can't do it. I kneel down and make it spin. He giggles, really loud.

Jay laughs.

"Sorry about the nappy!" I say but Jay just shrugs in a sort of 'didn't even notice it way' and he bends down to watch the spinner.

Gran hobbles back with the milk and puts it on the hall table.

"I was just thinking, Jay, you and Amy must be about the same age."

We both nod.

"We were at Ashleigh together, Gran."

Gran looks at me as if I've just said we were both in the same space shuttle that blasted off to Mars last week.

"Well, I never!" says Gran. "Fancy that! What a shame you're not going to the same high school."

"Well," I say. "Actually we're both down for Thornberry, Gran. For now at least." I turn back to look at Jay. I feel bad for making it sound as if I don't want to go there but he isn't listening. He is making the top spin, faster and faster. Maxi is bouncing up and down, dribbling and giggling.

"Oh, how wonderful!" says Gran. "That's such great news. And both of you here together this week."

"What's great news?" Mum flies in from behind, eager

to hear this incredible announcement.

Gran beams at her, holding her crutches high as if the sticks of plastic should join in the fun too.

"This is Jay. Paul's son from across the road."

"Hi, Jay," says Mum. "Don't you…"

"Jay's going to Thornberry too!" says Gran.

I don't like where this is going.

"That's amazing!" says Mum.

Yes, truly amazing, Mum, that two kids should be going to the same high school.

"Maybe…" says Mum. Oh no, please don't, Mum… "You and Amy could get to know each other a bit better this week." She's done it. Of course she has.

I stare at the floor. A drip of sweat drops from my armpit. Poor Jay. Being thrown in with me and my mangled hair.

Sam yells that he can't find his binoculars.

Jay smiles and shrugs. Gran picks up the milk and passes it to him.

He goes to speak but nothing comes. He taps his studs as if the action might help. Bits of mud flick on to Gran's path and hit the stone hedgehog by the front door. He bends down and wipes them off, brushes them into the border. I like the way he does that. And then he stands up and says, "Thanks," and he turns and runs back across the road.

"Such a nice lad," says Gran, closing the door. "Very quiet, bless him. I gave him his football back once because it had flown across the road and he just took it and didn't say anything. Just very shy, I think."

I want to say something, to tell them why Jay is so quiet, but I can't think of the right words.

Mum scoops up Maxi. He's holding the spinner but then he drops it and it clatters to the floor.

"I think I should have chosen the cuddly toy," says Gran. I pick up the spinner and pass it to Mum and then Sam bursts past us, opens the door and runs on to the front path.

"They're still there! Look!" he yells. I wander outside again and look up. The sky is a blanket of grey behind the two giant birds.

And then I look back across at Jay's house. Jay is in the lounge, stroking the cat curled up on the windowsill.

"They circle to hide from their prey," says Sam, his head tilted up, binoculars stuck to his eyes. "They can spot prey up to a mile away, Ames, did you know that?"

"No," I say. "I didn't." Jay looks out, sees us, lifts a hand to wave.

"They've gone," says Sam and he goes indoors.

I wave at Jay and go back inside and rub the towel

against my hair and wonder how Jay feels about going to Thornberry.

He seems fine about it.

I wish I did.

Thirteen

Dad is trying to FaceTime while we eat dinner but Mum's signal isn't strong enough.

"I'll have to see if that Wi-Fi box still works," says Gran.

Yes, yes. Please put the Wi-Fi back on.

"No, Dad will just pull the lead out again," says Mum. "And it needs replacing. There's a dent where it got dropped." She turns back to Dad's blurry face on her phone. "We'll try and call you tomorrow, love. Everyone yell bye to Dad." We all shout 'bye'.

"Do you still have the box, Gran?" I ask.

Mum glares at me. "No," she says. "We've enough to deal with."

"OK, OK," I say. I cut into my fish and stab a chip. "Only asking. No need to bite my head off."

Mum cuts a few chips into tiny bits and puts them on Maxi's plate.

"I was thinking," says Gran. "Would you like to have Jay over this week, Amy?"

I shove a huge forkful of food into my mouth. Oh my God. I can feel Mum look up, a little smile on her face, glancing from me to Gran, as if she's not sure how this will go.

"If you're both going to Thornberry…"

"Gran," I snap, a piece of cod escaping on to my lip. I lick it back in. "I'm fine, thanks. And I'm going to Valley High, remember. I won't see Jay again after this week."

"Oh," says Gran. "I thought that was looking more and more un—"

Mum puts her cutlery down with a clatter and shakes her head at Gran.

Gran sips her juice, shifts her ankle. "Of course," she says. "Sorry, I wasn't thinking."

No, neither were my parents, Gran, when they moved house. I shake the ketchup bottle hard and squirt it on my chips.

We eat in silence. Maxi squirms in his seat.

"I need help tying the trap cam to the tree," says Sam. "I couldn't do it on my own."

"I'll help," I say, taking the last mouthful. Brill. Good old Sam. I can get away from talking about schools and having Jay round. I really don't think Jay will want to come round.

"If we do it now. Can we get down?"

"Why the rush?" says Pops. He's staring at his food, wiping the chips in the mushy peas, coating each one so they look green.

"Don't do that, love," says Gran. She reaches out with one hand and lays it on his arm but he flicks her away. She sits back. We all wait a moment.

Gran wipes her hands on her serviette, moves the salt pot, tries to smile.

"Pops is just a bit tired, that's all. Been a busy day today. You two, go and sort the trap cam," she says. "I'll come and see it when you're done." Sam gets up and gives her a little hug.

"You can be the test badger," he says.

Maxi shouts and grabs a clump of chips from his high chair and throws them back down, banging his little white table. Pops stares at him hard.

"Who is that?" he says.

"Come on," I say to Sam and we take our plates to the sink and go out to the garden.

"He doesn't know Maxi," says Sam.

"He forgets," I say. "It's part of Pops now. Mum says he forgets recent things mostly and Maxi is recent to him."

Sam fiddles with the camera strap, tries to untangle it.

"I don't like it," he says.

"I know," I say, pulling at the knots on the long end. "I know. But we have to just treat him the same."

Sam nods and sniffs and I hold the camera in place while he wraps the strap around the tree.

"What are you hoping to see?" I ask. Sam looks up and stares at me a bit. I've never asked before. I'm not usually interested.

"Um… Well, the dormouse *obviously*. It needs to be higher though, I think. They live up in the trees and bushes. And Gran has a hedgehog that comes in the garden. That would be cool."

Gran comes out, her crutches tapping on the patio.

"Right, I'm badger-ready," she says and we laugh as she hobbles over and waves her crutches in front of the camera lens.

Fourteen

Pops is the jigsaw king. We sit in the morning sunshine and do it together. We have a system, me and Pops, that we've always used. I find the similar-coloured pieces, Pops fits them so quickly I can't quite keep up. We're doing our favourite 1000-piece. The picture is a really cosy cottage nestled in the woodlands with a river flowing past and a huge sunset sky. I'm jigging Maxi on my lap, while I find the bits. He reaches out and slaps the table and two pieces fall to the ground.

"Mum," I shout, but quietly with a hiss, trying not to break the pattern we are in. Luckily, she's right outside, carrying a pile of laundry. She puts her head round the door and I glare at her, nod my head at the jigsaw to show me and Pops are busy and Maxi is being a pain. She dumps the laundry and scoops him up.

Pops turns to Mum, holds a jigsaw piece of sky very still in his hand and then he says, "Let's all go to the pub for lunch, shall we?" He looks back down and slots the piece in.

Mum is staring at Pops, trying to decide what to say. "Not sure Mum can walk that far, Dad."

"Course she can," says Pops. "It's only on the corner." It's true. The pub is on the corner. "I'll go get ready."

"Bit early yet," says Mum. "And Gran's physiotherapist is coming round. She should be here soon."

"Let's finish the sky first," I suggest.

Mum makes a sign to me to keep busy on the jigsaw. She mouths, '*He'll forget*.'

We keep fitting pieces in. There is orange sky and blue sky and pink sky. We find the pieces for the river and the log pile. Gran's physiotherapist calls round and when she leaves we are still going.

"So many shades," says Pops. "So much sky." But at last the pieces are in and the jigsaw is nearly done. Just the cottage left.

Pops stands up.

"Let's finish this later," he says. "After lunch. I'm going to get ready. They do the best scampi at the pub, Amy. Do you like scampi?"

I look up at him and nod and then I go to find Mum and Gran and tell them that he's gone upstairs to get ready.

"Oh blimey," says Mum. "OK, I'm sure it will be fine. Do us all good."

We gather in the hall, Gran on her crutches, Maxi strapped into his stroller, Sam clutching his trap cam.

"Do you think you should bring that?" says Mum. "What if you drop it or something spills on it?"

Sam just shrugs and keeps hold of it.

For a moment we think Pops has forgotten but then he comes down in his jacket and tie and opens the little drawer in the hall. He pulls out his wallet.

"My treat," he says. "You've been such a help to us with Gran and her bad ankle." He takes Gran's arm and we close the door and walk down the road, Gran's crutches tapping on the pavement, Maxi leaning out of his stroller, trying to catch the leaves on the hedgerow.

❧ ❧ ❧

Pops insists we all order scampi. The waitress is worried the chef doesn't have enough. She spends a long time checking.

Sam scrolls through his camera footage while we wait, showing Gran every bit of film. She's excellent on the first badger and second pigeon but by the third cat, she looks a bit tired. Sam flicks his eyes from the camera to her face, checking she's still paying attention.

The waitress comes with the scampi on a giant tray. Gran looks a little relieved.

"I'll see more later," she says and checks we all have cutlery.

We dig in and agree with Pops that the scampi is the best. Maxi has little bits, all cut up on his tray. Mum has some Cheerios on hand in case he doesn't like it. But he does. He stuffs the scampi in, making a loud humming sound as he chews, as if he's never eaten anything so tasty.

Pops stares at him.

"He likes it," he says. "That baby, he loves the scampi. He's making that humming noise, like you used to, love, with tomatoes." He points at Mum and makes the noise.

"I'm sure I wasn't *that* loud!" Mum laughs.

"You were!" says Pops, smiling. "With tomatoes, every time," and he hums again. We all laugh. It's nice hearing Pops remember things. But then Pops hums even louder and the lady on the table next to us glances over and smiles, like you would smile at a child. I don't like it.

"Yes, love," says Gran, putting her hand on his arm. "Always with tomatoes."

The waitress comes back and we all order ice cream. Pops gets confused by the list of flavours.

"I'd like all of them," he says to the girl, slapping his menu down on the table.

"Um," she says. "We only really do three scoops. And there are ten flavours to choose from." She shakes her pen around. Mum says that's fine and she'll come and see her in a minute. I don't like that much either. I don't want the waitress to think Mum is treating Pops like a child.

"I'm thirsty," says Pops.

"I'll get more drinks," says Mum, scattering chocolate buttons on Maxi's highchair to keep him busy. He stuffs one in and hums again.

"See if they have biscuits," says Pops.

"OK," says Mum. I go with her to the bar to help carry everything.

When we get back, Gran is watching Sam's camera shots again. She looks up, pleased to see us.

"I'll enjoy the rest later," she says, tapping Sam on his arm and taking her juice from the tray.

And then we all realize Pops isn't there.

Mum rushes to the door of the pub and looks down the street. She's a bit breathless when she comes back. "Can't see him," she says.

"Oh!" says Gran, lifting both hands to her face. "I bet he's gone to the loo. He'll know where they are. We've been here so often. But he can't do that."

"Why?" says Sam.

Gran and Mum are staring at each other.

"He forgets how the locks work," says Gran. "He was stuck in the garden centre for an hour last time we went."

Mum darts to the toilets and Gran hobbles behind on her crutches. I can just see them, round the corner. Maxi is restless so I lift him out and plonk him on my lap. He's covered in melted yuck. I sing gently to him while I wipe his face with a wet wipe. He reaches for my hair. He smells of chips and scampi and chocolate and dribble.

They try the men's door. It's locked. Gran calls Pops' name and taps on the door with one of her crutches. They look at each other and back at us. Mum pulls her hand through her hair. And then the door starts to open and they both sink a little with relief.

Pops comes out carrying a large, framed painting of a stag.

I can't hear what they're saying but there's a lot of pointing and gasping and Gran tries to take the picture back. Mum charges over to me.

"Get Sam. He wants to show Sam."

I nudge Sam and tell him what's happening. He goes over to Pops and looks at the painting and they talk about the stag and the antlers. Pops seems happy. But then a man walks past me and goes towards the toilets. He wants to use the loo. Pops is standing right by the door, holding the painting. He won't let him in. Gran tries to pull him out of the way. And then Pops shouts, quite loudly, "It needs to go back," and he turns back into the toilet and I see Mum jam her foot in between the door so he can't shut the door and lock it.

The man takes a step back and gets out his phone while he waits. I hug Maxi and we sing 'Wheels on the Bus'. The man puts his phone away and checks his watch. And then they all come out and return to the table and Mum takes Maxi from me.

"I'll read to him," says Mum and she grabs a book from the stroller.

The bowls of ice cream arrive covered in cream, chocolate sauce and a flake.

"How many flavours?" says Pops.

"All of them," says Mum, looking at us to check we know not to comment.

"Best ice creams we had," says Pops, licking his spoon, "were on that beach, Suzie, down in St Margaret's Bay, remember?"

Gran nods and smiles. "Of course I remember," she says.

"They had tiny pink and white marshmallows and those sprinkles that come in all the colours." We all stare at Pops and listen. "And you spilled yours down your new silk blouse."

"And you wiped it up for me, love," says Gran. "With your hanky." He nods and we all eat quietly. We scrape the bowls clean. Pops picks his up and licks it. Sam laughs and copies him but Mum tells him to stop. The waitress comes back to take the empty bowls. Pops won't hand his over. He just keeps licking the bowl, turning it round and round, his hands grasping the edge. It's not funny any more. Gran tries to take it. Pops holds it tight. Maxi is watching. He starts to giggle. Mum grabs a different book and holds it in front of Maxi's face but he bats it away and watches again, laughing. No one knows what to do. And then Sam taps Pops and says, "Can I show you my camera now?"

"Yes, please, I'd like that," says Pops. He puts the bowl down hard and it clatters and rocks and the spoon falls to the floor. The waitress picks it up and takes away our bowls and glasses.

"Well done, Sam," mutters Gran.

Pops puts on his glasses and watches as the recordings flash.

"Extraordinary," he says. "Incredible … well, I never … stunning!"

Pops is a very, very good watcher.

A friend of Gran's comes over to chat. There is lots of oohing and aahing about her ankle.

I get out my phone and log in to the pub's Wi-Fi.

"Phone away, love," says Mum.

But Gran taps Mum's arm and says, "It's fine. We've finished eating."

I give Gran a little smile and look at my phone but then I wish I hadn't because I'm still in the cinema group chat for today and they're all planning what food to buy and what to wear and what film to watch.

My little scabies friends pop up.

I put my phone away.

"When are we leaving?" I ask Mum.

"Soon," she says.

I slump back, kick my legs out, fold my arms.

"What's wrong?" she asks, pointing to the dinosaur on the page for Maxi.

I shake my head, look away, my lips tight.

"Don't get in a grump," says Mum. She turns back to the book and Maxi. I shake my head from side to side and imitate her, mouthing the words. I hate it when she says I'm in a grump. It makes me sound like I'm a toddler.

The waitress comes over with the bill. Gran nudges Pops and says, "You wanted to pay, love, didn't you?" but he looks at her blankly and then turns back to Sam's screen. "Never mind, I've got it," says Gran, getting out her purse.

"I'll get ours," says Mum but Gran insists on treating us.

She turns to me. "Did you enjoy it, Amy?" and as it's Gran asking, I sit up and smile and say it was delicious.

We stand up to go. We sort of tumble out of the pub, bags falling from the bottom of the stroller and Gran's crutches catching on the door on the way out. I can see the waitress smile a bit and I don't like it. I grab Gran's arm and help her out of the door.

"Nuisance, these things," she says, tapping the crutches hard. We gather outside, waiting for Mum to strap Maxi in properly. My phone beeps. I get it out of my pocket. It's a photo of the girls outside the cinema, clutching smoothies. There are five of them. Cassie, Molly and Sophia. I stare at the other two. I'm not sure who they are. And then I see the beads and the nails and I realize it's the two girls from the District Sports event, the ones from their form at Valley High. Zoe and Sara or whatever they're called.

It's like they're all getting closer and closer and I'm moving further away. They'll probably forget about me soon. I'll be 'that girl Amy who used to live near here'.

I shove my phone back into my pocket.

Gran is watching me. I try to look less grumpy but it's impossible right now. It's like the scabies have taken over me, chasing round inside, sending little irritable messages to every part of my body.

"Do you know what?" says Gran. "I've just remembered we've run out of teabags. Amy, would you mind going to the shop for me and picking some up, and some sweets for you and Sam and more chocolate buttons for his lordship." She nods to Maxi who is now looking sleepy in his stroller.

"She doesn't need to," says Mum.

"The shop is only there," says Gran, nodding at the corner shop next to the pub. "Amy's eleven now. She's fine to just buy teabags and sweets and follow us home." She tucks two notes into my hand and leans in to me and whispers, "Sorry you've got to miss out right now."

"It doesn't matter, Gran," I say and I feel bad that she's noticed my mood, especially when she was treating us.

She takes Pops' arm and hobbles away. The others follow and I turn and walk towards the shop.

Fifteen

A car pulls up just ahead of me. I recognize it straight away this time. The door opens and Jay jumps out. He's in his football kit. He puts his ear pods in his pocket and runs straight inside, his studs tapping on the concrete, bits of mud flying off. His dad drives away, beeping the horn just once, as if to say bye.

I'm not sure what to do. It seems a bit odd following Jay in but then a group of teenagers spin up on their bikes. They're swearing and arguing and I feel uneasy and out of place so I scuttle inside.

The shop is small and cramped but every shelf is bulging.

I dash into the middle aisle, searching for teabags. There are cans and cereals and pasta but no teabags.

"Can I help you, love?" says a lady stacking shelves.

"Um, teabags, please," I say. Two of the teenagers have followed me in.

"Round here," she says and I follow her to a different

aisle. It leads to the tills. Jay is in the queue. I find the teabags and grab the nearest box. The teenage lads brush past me and take drinks from a fridge. The sweets are just further along so I find some chocolate buttons and two packets of pastilles and wait to pay. A lady is at the front, then Jay, then the two big lads, then me.

The lady pays and leaves. Jay puts his drink and snacks on the counter. The guy behind the till puts the things in a carrier bag and tells him how much. Jay rustles in his pocket and lays out the coins he has.

"Not quite enough, mate," says the guy called '*Connor, here to help*'.

Jay stares at him, looks down at the coins, stares back at him. Jay says nothing. The whole shop seems silent, the queue all waiting, watching.

"You need another ninety pence," says Connor.

The two lads in between us start shifting a bit, shuffling forward as if moving nearer the counter will make Jay hurry.

"Maybe put something back?" says Connor.

Jay nods, turns to look at the door, as if hoping to see his dad. His cheeks are bright red.

"Which thing?" says Connor. "Tell me and I'll get it out of the bag." He says it as if he doesn't trust Jay, as if Connor is the only one who can choose the item. I'm not sure Connor is really *here to help*. The teenagers smile at each other as if this is funny. Jay says nothing. And then I realize that I don't think he can. I think his words are stuck. So then I do it. I just do it. I don't even think about it. I move forward, slide past the two lads, say 'excuse me' in a tiny voice and pass Jay a fiver.

"Your dad gave me this," I say. "He saw me come in and thought you wouldn't have enough."

Jay nods and passes Connor the fiver and everything is quickly sorted. He flies out of the shop, super quick.

The boys in front move forward. I look at the money I have left and jog back to check the price of the teabags and the buttons. I can't afford the pastilles now so I change them for one little fudge bar. No sweets for me today but it really doesn't matter.

I pay and then dash outside.

Jay is waiting, leaning against the wall, staring at his boots.

He looks up.

"Hi," he says, taking his ear pods out. "Here's your change, thanks." He passes me the coins. "I'll pay you back later."

"No need," I say, glancing at him.

"Did … did you have enough?" he says.

"Yeah, plenty thanks," I say. We walk side by side, back

past the pub and towards our road. The sun is hot now, bouncing off the concrete path. I want to take my cardigan off but I don't.

"I-I thought the crisps were half price," says Jay.

"I do that all the time," I say. "Once, I had to put everything back."

Jay smiles.

"Did you play football again today?" I ask.

No, Amy, he just wears his kit for fun.

But Jay just nods. There are a few seconds' silence and then he says, "Yeah, it goes into next week."

"Is that with Josh, for the county squad?"

"Yeah," he says. "One of these summer camps."

We're soon back home standing in the street, our houses either side of the road.

"I like your cat," I say, nodding over to Jay's lounge windowsill. The cat is looking out at the front hedge, paws tucked under.

"That's Captain," says Jay. "We only got him a few weeks ago so he has to stay inside until he knows this is his home."

"Cool."

My phone buzzes in my pocket. I move my hand to get it. But I change my mind. It's probably Cassie. I didn't answer her last message and she won't like that.

Jay picks up the basketball, bounces it a few times on the path.

"Want to shoot a few hoops?" he says.

"OK," I say, laughing. "I'm not very good, though."

"Doesn't matter," says Jay.

"I'll just take these in." I lift up the teabags and sweets.

Jay nods.

I run inside and dump the shopping and go to the loo.

"You OK, Amy?" shouts Mum.

"Yep," I say. "I'll just be out front for a bit."

"I'll come," calls Sam, running to the lounge door.

"No, you won't," I yell.

"What are you doing?" shouts Mum. She's coming this way, towards the hall so I dash outside and close the door fast.

I don't need Mum asking questions and being all bustly and happy right now that I am shooting hoops with someone going to Thornberry.

Sixteen

"Sorry I'm so bad," I say. I chase my missed shot and pass it back to Jay. I'm worried I'm going to have sweat patches through my cardie soon. Jay smiles and bounces the ball. I can tell he wants to say something. It's the way his mouth moves, just a little bit.

"I-it takes practice," he says. "And Dad set the ring at full height. Most hoops are set lower."

We pass the ball and shoot a few more hoops and then Jay stops and offers me crisps from the giant packet he bought.

I take one and hold the packet while he shoots again.

"Do you like Thornberry?" I ask, biting the crisp and feeling the spice on my tongue.

"Yeah," he says, bouncing the ball. "It's great. The sport's the best around." He scores a hoop from way down the drive.

"Oh," I say. I wasn't expecting him to sound quite so keen.

"And I'm lucky. A few of my mates are going from my old primary school. And my cousin."

"Oh," I say again. I thought we shared this thing about knowing no one at Thornberry.

He goes to say something but it doesn't come out so he bounces the ball again and shoots. Then he turns back to me.

"Which form are you in?" he says.

I take another crisp and bite hard. The spice makes my mouth tingle.

"I don't know. I'm still hoping for Valley High."

"Oh," he says.

"Yeah, my parents promised." I look over at Gran's house.

Jay bounces the ball again, over and over. "My parents split up. That's why I came to Ashleigh. Mum and me moved nearby so I went there."

I dig for another crisp.

"My dad had an accident," I say. "A bad one. He couldn't work for a long time. We had to move too. The new house is miles away. That's why I can't go to Valley High."

"Tough," says Jay. I nod.

"These are *so* nice," I say, looking at the packet. Thai sweet chilli.

"The best," says Jay and he passes me the ball and it crushes the crisps and we both laugh.

"Thai sweet bashed-up chilli," I say.

Jay's dad comes out to get something from his car.

"Hi," he says to me. "I'm Paul, Jay's dad." I smile and wave. "You must be Amy. Jay said you were staying over the road with your gran." I glance at Jay. I'm pleased he told his dad. Jay turns and shoots.

"Go OK in the shop?" says Paul, looking at Jay for the answer.

Jay nods and shrugs. He catches the ball and bounces it hard, scowls at his dad a little but Paul is already heading back inside.

I wonder why he asked him that. Maybe he knew he might not have enough money.

Jay's phone beeps in his pocket. He takes it out and reads the message.

"Gotta go. Sorry. I…" There is a gap, a pause. "I'm gaming with Josh at five thirty."

I think *I* is a hard word for Jay.

"OK," I say and I pass him the crisp packet back. We say bye and then I run back across the street and ring the doorbell. Sam opens the door.

"I hate fudge," he says, holding up the bar I bought him in the shop.

"Oh, don't moan," I say and I shove past him.

"You know I hate fudge!" he shouts.

Pops calls me. I join him in the front room. He's looking out across the road, at Jay's house. "That young man," he says. "Spitting image of my old mate Spinney. Does he have a grandpa called Spinney?"

"Um, I don't know, Pops, I'll ask him."

"Yes, do," says Pops.

"When were you mates with Spinney?" I look at him closely. I want to hear more.

"Gosh. Years ago." He smiles and drags his hand down his face, pulls on his chin, as if the memories are flooding back. "Me and Spinney were at school together and then became apprentices at the same time. Best joiner you ever saw, old Spinney. His dovetail joints were sublime. And then we'd spend hours down the pub playing the board."

"What game was that?" I ask.

He spins round and stares at me, his eyes wide.

"What game?" he says. "Well, it would hardly be chess, would it?"

"I don't know, Pops," I say.

"I'll show you," he says. But then he sits down in his chair and closes his eyes and smiles, chanting a little to himself, "*Spinney, Spinney, shove that ha'penny, winny, winny.*"

I kiss his cheek and leave the room, closing the door softly. Sam is waiting for me, holding up the fudge bar.

"You know I wanted pastilles," he says. "And why couldn't I come out front earlier?" He stares at me. He can make a big deal of things, Sam. And I do feel bad for snapping at him when he wanted to join us outside. So I grab the fudge out of his hand, yell to Mum that I'm going back to the shop and I fly out of the door and run down the road, the coins Jay gave me jangling in my pocket.

❧ ❧ ❧

Maxi has chocolate all round his mouth, all down his front.

"What a sight!" says Gran, laughing. "Good job your bath is running, young man."

The teabags I bought are still on the side so I put them in the cupboard. Gran has two spare boxes. I think she used the teabags as an excuse. She knew I was feeling fed up. Gran's clever like that.

I wander outside. Sam is at the bottom of the garden, tying up the trap cam.

"Thanks for the pastilles," he mutters like a robot, as if he doesn't really want to say thanks. He can't wrap the strap around the tree and keep the trap cam in place. He gets frustrated, kicks the ground as the strap falls again. "Can you just hold this for me?" He passes me the trap cam. "Got nothing last night. Nothing."

My phone beeps in my pocket. I take it out with my spare hand. It's Molly.

That Zoe girl is not so nice ☹ **... Miss u x**

There is a line of sad face emojis.

That makes me feel kind of glad, the bit about Zoe. But none of this is Molly's fault. I text her back.

Miss u 2 see u soon xxx

Dad has messaged too. A photo of him standing on the full skip, arms up like Popeye showing his muscles, pulling a face like he's on the loo. It makes me laugh.

Sam is still struggling.

"Why are you tying it here?" I say to him. "It's so overgrown." He looks up.

"This bit, where the hazel tree is, backing on to the woodland, is a perfect hazel dormouse habitat." He pulls the strap and I take the long end from him to wrap it around the trunk.

"Isn't this a bit high for a mouse?" I ask.

Sam sighs. "They live in the trees. They're really hard to spot." And then he pushes a few buttons and looks at me with slanted eyes. "Why are you suddenly being so helpful?"

I shrug.

I help him tie the trap cam and then I show him Dad's photo. He laughs, very loudly, and puts his arms up too, biceps on show.

We lie down on the grass and stare at the blue sky and the birds and the clouds. "Dad and I always look for shapes," I say. "What can you see?"

Sam is quiet for a moment and then he points and says, "Well, that one looks like a sheep."

I laugh. "Sam, they're fluffy white clouds! They *all* look like sheep."

"But that…" says Sam, sitting up and pointing, "is a real live goldfinch!" He follows the little yellow flash as it flies across the garden and disappears over the hedge next door.

Seventeen

The kitchen is covered in flour. We seem to have been baking all afternoon. Gran makes brilliant cakes but it's hard with her ankle so she's had to talk me through it from her chair and I've got a bit muddled.

"It gets easier each time," says Gran. "You made them yourself, that's the main thing." We ice the cakes, each of them flatter than the last.

I start to wash up. The amount of bowls and gooey spoons seems crazy when all we have are twelve flat fairy cakes.

"I'm going for a quick lie-down upstairs," says Gran. "Keep an ear out for Pops will you, Amy love? He's in the front room. Mum should be back soon with the boys from the park."

"No probs," I say.

I'm just finishing up when there is a knock on the front door.

"That'll be your mum," shouts Gran from her room.

"Just a sec!" I yell and I wash the last bowl and peel off the gloves.

"Suzie!" yells Pops from the hall. "Suzie!"

I rush out to him. "It's OK, Pops," I say. "It's just Mum, that's all. With the boys." He nods a little and leans on the windowsill, knocking a picture frame to the floor. I pick it up and open the door. It's not Mum. It's Jay, holding a pint of milk.

"Hi," he says, smiling. "Dad sent this. To replace the pint we borrowed."

Pops moves beside me. He stares at Jay. He stares hard.

"Well, I never," he says.

"You OK, Pops?" I say. "This is Jay from over the road. Paul's son."

"Spinney," says Pops. "Hello, my dear friend." He reaches out and shakes Jay's hand, over and over.

"Hi," says Jay.

"You are Spinney, aren't you?"

"Um, no." Silence. Jay looks down at his feet. He can't find the words.

"Well, who are you then, lad? Speak up!"

I freeze a bit, my eyes going wide. "I just said, Pops, this is Jay."

But Pops ignores me, doesn't hear me.

"I'm sorry," I say to Jay quietly. "He doesn't understand."

Pops hears that.

"Who doesn't understand?" he says, barking at me. And then he spins back to Jay. "Who are you?"

"Jay, sir. My name is Jay." It's sweet how he uses 'sir'. I think Pops likes it.

"Well," says Pops, shuffling his feet and rubbing his head. "You are the spit of my good friend Spinney. Have you come for a game, young man?"

"Sorry?" says Jay.

"A game, come on. Let's see if we can get the old board out."

He wanders back through the house.

"I've no idea what he's talking about," I whisper. "He has a few memory problems." And then I feel bad for saying that, as if I've let Pops down. I don't know if he wants people to know.

"No worries," says Jay.

Pops stops and turns back to us both.

"Come on!" he shouts. "I'm waiting!"

"Shall I come in?" says Jay.

I nod. "If that's OK with you?"

Jay looks back across the driveway and shouts to his

dad. Paul is standing by the front door, tapping away on his phone.

"I'm just going to Amy's for a bit!"

I like the way he says that. Like we're friends.

His dad waves and shouts back, "OK. Hi, Amy! Don't be long. We're going out in half an hour."

Jay follows me through the house. He stops for a moment and looks at all the things lining the shelves in the hall. He stops to stroke the wooden owl.

"This is amazing!" he says.

"Pops carved it, when I was little."

"Wow," says Jay and he looks closer and I smile and feel so proud of Pops.

In the shed, Pops puts on the radio and the lights. He picks up a chisel and a piece of wood. Jay is looking around him, staring at all the frames and bowls and half-finished projects.

I move to Pops and lay my hand on his arm.

"Pops, you wanted to show Jay the game?"

"What game?" he says.

"The game you played with Spinney."

Pops puts the chisel down. He looks out of the little shed window and says, "*Spinney, spinner, you mighty winner! Coins fly so fast, they get ten times thinner!*" He beams a smile at me, his eyes super wide. "Haven't sung that for a few years!"

"What game was it? Maybe a card game? Or draughts?"

And then Pops looks at Jay and makes this silly face as if to say, 'What's she like?'

"Hear that, Spinney?" he says. "What *game* was it?"

He laughs hard. And then he starts pulling things out of the shelving area, ducking behind counters.

"It's here somewhere, I'm sure."

"What are you looking for, Pops?" I ask. "Can we help?"

Very soon, the shed floor is covered in planks of wood and toolboxes and old framing materials. Jay has to step back against the door. Pops is down on his hands and knees, dragging something out from behind some old paint cans. I'm starting to feel a bit panicky, as if I need to get Gran. Jay bends down and piles up some of the wood.

"Here we go," says Pops. "Look, Spinney, here it is." I let out a long breath, like I've been holding it until he found what he was searching for. He pulls out a large, flat box, about the size of our biggest jigsaw.

"Pops," I say, helping him up. I look at him and say quite firmly, "This isn't Spinney, this is Jay. Jay Parker from across the road."

He glances at Jay again with that *Who is this girl?* look

and says, "OK, OK, calm down. Nice to meet you, Jay." And he puts his hand out and shakes Jay's hand again. "Now let's have a game."

The box is covered in brown paper and tied with string. He unwraps it and lays out a large wooden board. It has a lip at the end that hooks on to the end of the workbench to keep it from slipping. There are thin lines across the board, like lanes in a swimming pool. Each row is long and even and straight. And then Pops opens a leather wallet and takes out five large coins.

"You played before, Amy?" asks Pops.

I shake my head.

Jay leans over, picks up a coin and turns it over in his hands.

"We'll have to show her then, young Jay," says Pops.

He starts to explain the game. The name, shove ha'penny. The coins being nudged down each lane. The skill involved. The fact the coins help each other. How you nudge the coin with the side of your hand. The way you use talc to keep the board smooth. How marks are chalked on the side.

"Let's play!" says Pops.

We each have a go, nudging the coins into the lanes. We ask lots of questions. Pops teaches us about a 'build' and what a 'perfect go' is. He tells us stories of matches down the pub. Of their great rivals from the Unicorn pub with their board of bog oak that was as slippy as ice. And then he stops and stands very still and it's as though he can't quite remember what he was saying or what we are doing.

There's a knock on the shed door. It's Jay's dad.

"Sorry to disturb you all. Susan said you were in here." He turns to Jay. "We need to go. We'll be late for dinner."

"OK," says Jay. "Thanks so much, Mr, um…" He's not sure what to call Pops.

"Call me Pops," says Pops and he turns to Paul. "Your lad is quite the superstar." Pops is right here, in the moment again.

"Ah, thanks," says Paul. "Yes, we're super proud of him. Especially with everything Jay has to … you know, cope with."

Jay looks up, turning a coin in his hand, glances at his dad, turns back to the board, his cheeks slightly pink. I don't think he liked what his dad just said.

But Pops hasn't noticed. "It's a good game, this."

"They need to go," I whisper to Pops.

"You should play!" says Pops, holding out a coin for Paul to take.

Paul takes a step forward, glances at his watch, peers into the shed. And then his eyes widen and he takes another step and he says, "I haven't seen a shove ha'penny board for a long while. Used to play with my old man." He picks up one of the coins and rubs it over the board, back and forth. Pops watches him, looks at me and nods as if he's helped someone else to go back in time. Which he has.

Paul's phone rings. He nudges the coin down one lane and then takes his phone out, swipes the screen and answers it.

"OK, on our way," he says. "Get them to keep the table." He ends the call and ruffles Jay's hair. "I'll back the car out. Hurry up, Jay!" He says thanks to Pops and runs off back through the house.

Jay turns to Pops. He stops and stares and looks down. And looks up again. And I'm so glad he persevered because then he says, "I-I loved the game, Pops. Could we play again?"

Pops smiles and picks up the coins, making them into a neat stack.

"Of course," he says. "I'll talc the board, ready for our next game."

"Shall I come tomorrow?" he says, looking at me. "After football?"

"Yeah, great," I say.

Jay smiles and turns and jogs away, lifting a hand to wave to me.

Pops and I watch him and then Pops very quietly chants, *"Spinner the winner, every time, Spinner the winner, rows in line."*

Eighteen

A screech downstairs wakes me. The camp bed has slightly collapsed this morning, the canvas middle sagging. I have to tip myself out of it. Sam is downstairs, yelling for Mum. It sounds like something's wrong. I heave myself up fast.

"Mum!" he screams. "I need you, *right now!*" I grab my dressing gown, reach for the door. Maybe Maxi fell or Pops has put something plastic in the oven again. Mum's footsteps run along the landing. I poke my head round the door to decide if I'm really needed.

"What is it?" yells Mum, leaning over the banister.

"Two hedgehogs! Two of them! Right by the camera! It slipped down the tree but that doesn't matter because I got hedgehogs!" He turns and runs back outside.

"Great," mutters Mum. "Woken up at seven a.m. to be told about two spiky mammals on the first day in weeks Maxi has slept past five." And then Maxi shouts from the travel cot and Mum pads back to her room, giving me a quick hug on the way.

"You OK, love?" she says.

"I was," I say and I turn back to my room and lie down on the sagging canvas. After a few minutes I hear Gran's crutches hobbling to the bathroom. And then Mum going downstairs with Maxi. I look at my phone. Molly has texted.

> **So sad u can't make the sleepover tomorrow** 😣

She's added a gif of a dopey puppy. I send a line of sad face emojis.

> **What u been doing?**

> **Not much. Jay Parker is living across the street with his dad.**

> **OMG no way!!!**

And then I wonder if I should have kept quiet. Once Cassie knows, it will be a real pain. So I add,

> **Don't tell Cass** 🤫

She sends a thumbs up and a heart.

♣ ♣ ♣

Jay knocks on the door at six. I'd been watching from the window, waiting. I run downstairs and open the door.

"Hi," I say.

"Is it still OK to come over?" he asks.

"Of course," I say. "Pops is in his shed, polishing the board. He's been talking about it all day!"

We go out into the garden. Sam is tying the trap cam on to a fencepost near to the bushes. Jay watches. He starts to speak but stops and walks a little closer to Sam.

"I-is that one of those nature cameras?" he asks.

"Yep," says Sam, pulling the strap tight. "I got two hedgehogs last night."

"Cool," says Jay. "Do they look for food together?"

"Nope," says Sam. "They're solitary nocturnal animals. I caught them at two different times. Two twenty five a.m. and four fifteen a.m."

"How do you know it wasn't the same hedgehog?" asks Jay.

Sam presses buttons on the screen. "Good question. One was bigger," he says.

Jay walks in front of the camera. "Does it respond to movement?" he asks.

Sam stops and looks at him. He wants to tell if he's really interested. Sam doesn't like people who waste his time. "Yes," he says. "And then it just takes a short film."

Jay nods. "What's the coolest animal you've ever caught?"

Sam sits back and thinks. "The badger was awesome."

"Wow," says Jay. "I don't think we get anything in our garden."

"You'd be surprised," says Sam and he checks the camera is on firmly. Jay is about to turn back when Sam adds, "I'm really hoping to catch the hazel dormouse. They're really hard to catch on camera and they aren't very common. They're endangered." He glances up, a little embarrassed, as if he's worried Jay won't be interested.

"I've never heard of one," says Jay. "What do they look like?" Sam tells Jay about their tiny bodies and long tails, their big eyes and soft golden fur. How they love to eat hawthorn and sleep nestled in the trees and that they aren't actually mice but rodents.

"Come on, you two," says Pops, standing at the door of his shed. "I'm going to teach you how to score today." He's holding a box of chalk. "Can be tricky."

We leave Sam with his camera and join Pops in the shed. The board is laid out ready, the coins lined up by the side.

"You go first," says Pops and Jay shoves the coin down the lane.

"It's perfect!" shouts Jay.

Pops leans in to look. He smiles and moves his head from side to side, as if he's not sure. "It's nearly perfect," he says. "Look, I think the coin is just over the edge. By a millimetre.

Amy, you'll have to adjudicate."

"What does that mean?" I ask.

"Be the judge, the referee, decide if the coin is clear."

I lean over the board, look carefully at the edge of the coin. Test if it's clear.

"I'd say it's fine."

Pops laughs and says, "OK, Spinney Jay, mark it up, you're a bit lucky there!" and he passes Jay the chalk. Jay marks the score on the side.

"There's a word for that move," says Pops, frowning. "When you get it straight away." He taps the chalk on his workbench. "What is it?" He can't think of it.

I watch them play, both of them intense, concentrating. And then it's my turn. Pops helps me but Jay wins easily. He plays Pops again and they have a long battle, each of them pulling coins back to go again. I look round Pops' shed, at all the stuff, all the half-finished projects, the tools, the machinery. I think of how much he knows. How much he can do. How he remembered that long judging word. Ajoodicay or whatever it was.

He remembers so much.

And then he remembers so little.

We are just finishing our last game when there's a knock on the shed door. It's Dad, Maxi in his arms, ready for bed. I didn't know he was coming over. He opens the door.

"Hey, love!" he says, hugging me. "Hi, Jay, how's it going?"

Jay smiles. "Good thanks," he says. "I-I was just about to go home."

"Don't leave because of me!" says Dad. Maxi leans over and pulls a hammer off the bench.

"Whoa!" I say, grabbing it back. "That is not for you, Maxi!"

"See you soon," says Jay, laughing at Maxi. "Bye, Pops," and he waves to everyone and runs out of the shed and back through the house.

Dad pats Pops on the back and hugs me hard. "You OK?" he says.

"Yep," I say.

"I'm glad Jay is over the road," he says, smiling.

"Yep."

"I hope me being here didn't spoil the game." He stops smiling, looks back after Jay, as if he should call him back. He has dots of white paint all over his face.

"No, it's fine," I say. I put the coins away and wipe the chalkboard clean.

"Good game that," says Pops.

Maxi nestles into Dad, his giraffe under his chin. We tidy the shed and when we leave the summer evening is settling in, a warm sunset sky over the house and it does feel good to have Dad here, to have his arm wrapped around me.

"I've bought a surprise," he says.

"Right," I say. "It's not that wallpaper, is it?"

"Nope." We open Gran's back door and the smell wafts towards me. The kitchen table is covered in boxes from our favourite chicken take-out.

"I got you spicy rice, you love that, right?"

I beam at him. "Just a bit!" I pinch a sneaky chip and Dad calls everyone and we all gather round the table and dig in, the chicken juicy and hot. Sam bites into his drumsticks, pulling away the meat and Gran laughs and says, "You look like a Viking, Sam! Let's all be Vikings. Pass the bucket round!"

Maxi screeches for a drumstick too but he can't have one so Mum cuts some up for him.

The kitchen is warm and cosy. Mum tells Dad about the scampi and the pub and how good it was.

"Pops showed me a stag," says Sam.

"Wow," says Dad.

"I didn't," says Pops. Sam starts to explain but Mum gently puts her hand on his and shakes her head. She hands him the chicken bucket and tells Dad about Maxi eating scampi and how he hummed and hummed.

"Yes," shouts Pops. "Like you, Julie, when you were little,

with tomatoes," and he does an impression of her and we all laugh and do the same with our chicken. When we stop, Maxi carries on, picking up the chicken, just like he did with the scampi, humming over and over.

I lean in to Dad. We are all together and happy, and I'm glad.

Nineteen

I'm woken up early *again*. Not by a screech this time but a bang. Like a door slamming.

I look outside. The road is quiet. Paul's car is still on their drive.

The bang worries me. Any bang in this house now worries us all. With Pops. So I grab my dressing gown.

The house is quiet. Which worries me even more. I pad downstairs. There are voices in the kitchen. I can hear Sam.

"Oh my God!" he yells. "A mouse, a mouse!" He flies past me and races upstairs, the trap cam in his hands. "I need to get my book to identify it."

I wrap my dressing gown tighter.

"Was that you at the door, Sam?" I want to throttle him.

"No, it was Jay. He came in the back door. It really bangs."

My feet stop but I'm already in the kitchen. And so is Jay. He's sitting at the kitchen table, holding a glass of juice in one hand and his phone in the other. There is a bowl of cereal in front of him. He's wearing his football kit. It's 7.35 in the morning.

What the…?

I wrap my dressing gown tighter.

"Hi," I say.

He raises one hand and smiles a little, takes out his ear pods. He looks a bit embarrassed. And a bit out of place sitting here so early. It's like the time I saw my dance teacher Jamila at the dentist. It was odd seeing her in jeans, flicking through a magazine.

"Do you need another pint of milk?" I ask.

He shakes his head.

"No, but do you have the Wi-Fi code?"

"Um," I say, not sure how to explain our Wi-Fi situation. "Not really."

And then Mum arrives, bustling in, whistling a tune, doing her 'happy house thing' she always does for visitors or the postman or delivery drivers. "There you are, Amy," she says. "I just went up to you, but you beat me down."

"Jay needs the Wi-Fi code," I say. Maybe she'll put the box back in now that Jay has asked. One dent is hardly a big problem.

"I-it doesn't matter," says Jay. He's nervous, I can tell. I'm not surprised with my mum bustling around him. He shifts in the chair. "I've texted Josh to say I'll be late."

"It's not working, Jay," says Mum. "I'm so sorry." She glares at me a little and I roll my eyes. She leaves and Sam walks in with his book.

"Bad news. It was just a field mouse. Cute, though." He holds up the book for me to see. There are lots of photographs of mice. Loads. Long tails, short tails, huge ears, tiny ears.

I've just woken up. Jay is in the kitchen. I'm looking at a page of mice. It's like some odd dream. I turn and leave, edging sideways. And then I tap up the stairs and find Mum. She is in her room, changing Maxi's nappy.

"How come Jay is here so early?" I say. "You could have told me."

"I tried to!" says Mum, dabbing cream on Maxi's behind. "I went to the loo and then came to tell you but you'd already gone downstairs. They have a gas leak, across the road. Paul rang to see if Jay could just come over and have some breakfast as they can't be in the house. Gas is very dangerous."

"How long is he going to be here for?"

"I don't know… Not long… Paul's sitting in his car arranging for the gas people to come round and then he'll take him to football. Nice lad. So shy, bless him." She pulls the tabs on the nappy and lifts Maxi on to her hip. "Come down and help me, Ames, please!"

She turns to go but then Gran calls from the bedroom that she can't reach her crutches. And then we both gasp a little as Pops walks past in just his underpants.

"Oh God," says Mum. She follows Pops and I go to my room and reach for my jeans and a sweatshirt and start to get dressed.

Twenty

We are sitting watching *Tom and Jerry*. I've got Maxi on my lap. He keeps staring at Jay, sucking on his fingers and then reaching over to Jay's face to touch him.

"I am *so* sorry," I say. "He can be really gross."

Jay just smiles.

"Bet he likes this," he says and he blows up his cheeks and then pops them with his hands like a burst balloon. Maxi stops and sits up and stares. Jay does it again and Maxi giggles. A third time and Maxi laughs so much he spits and it lands on Jay's cheek.

"Sorry … again…" I say and I take a tissue from the box on the table and pass it to Jay.

The cartoon finishes.

"I think there might be other DVDs," I say, reaching down to the basket beside me. I bring up *Snow White*, *Cinderella* and the *Garden Gnome's Christmas Show*. Jay laughs.

"I love *Tom and Jerry*," he says. He picks up the new remote control from Pops' table. He turns it over and then puts it down again, lining it up next to the clock.

I don't want him thinking it's stupid.

"It's new," I say.

He nods.

"It helps," I say. I don't want to say why. Although I think Jay must know by now. You spend time with Pops and you know pretty fast.

"My…" says Jay and he stops and moves the control and starts again. "My gran has the same one at the care home where she lives. She calls it her magic wand." I smile. We both look back at the new cartoon about to start. The lady's legs waddle across the screen, her stockings falling low. And then the DVD sticks, Tom's face frozen as he is about to pounce. The room goes very quiet. Maxi points at the screen.

"Did it smell bad?" I say.

Jay looks at me and says, "What? The controller?"

Why did I say *that*? I wanted to say something. Just so the room wasn't so quiet. But why my brain and my mouth decide on things like that I don't know.

"The gas. I've heard it smells really bad."

"Oh, yeah," he laughs. "It was disgusting."

"I saw this funny thing on TV once where they say that

gas doesn't actually smell. They put chemicals in it to make it smell. That way you know there's a leak."

I am *so* interesting.

"Oh," says Jay. "Well, it worked." Maxi reaches for him again so he does the popping cheek thing and Maxi collapses in giggles.

Jay's phone rings. He answers it.

"Yep…? Nope… *No*, Dad, I'm not doing that." He stands up and walks to the window, signals to his dad through the glass, shakes his head firmly. I sit up a little. I can see Paul standing by the car, talking into his phone and looking straight at Jay. "Why would I want to *do* that…? I know it's only Josh's mum but you know… I hate it and it *doesn't* help."

I've never seen Jay mad before. He mutters a bad word, turns his phone off, puts it in his pocket and sits back down and stares at the frozen TV. His arms are wrapped around his chest and he is breathing hard, in and out. He makes a little gulping sound, like he's trying not to cry.

"Let's take you to Mum," I say to Maxi and I carry him to the kitchen. When I'm back, Jay is better. He's calmer. He's checking his messages. Tom and Jerry are trying to chase, the picture sticking, trying to move on.

"Sorry," he says. "I hope I didn't upset Maxi."

"No," I say. "Maxi doesn't notice anything like that. Just as well in this house." I sit down and look at the screen but I'm not really watching. "And I get mad with my parents all the time," I say. "Don't worry about it."

"I-I-I've not heard back from Josh so Dad thinks he hasn't seen my text. He wanted me to phone Josh's mum about being late. To make sure the coach knows."

"Oh," I say. "Do you need her number? I could get it from Cass."

Jay is quiet for a moment, sits back on the sofa, kicks his legs out. "It's not that. He thinks it helps. He gives me stuff like that. Like asking for the milk. And going to the shop."

I sit down on the sofa.

"Oh," I say.

"It doesn't help."

"Oh."

"I don't need to do things like that."

"No, of course."

"I'm fine as I am."

I nod. The cartoon has started back up and is in full chase mode. The lady comes in with the broom held high, about to whack Jerry. I take the pastilles that I bought from the shop out of my pocket. I offer one to Jay and he takes it.

"Thanks," he says and we both laugh as Jerry dashes out

from under the broom and Tom gets the full whack on his head, those cartoon spirals coming out of his head.

Twenty-one

The cartoon ends. Jay's dad knocks on the window and points at the front door. We get up and walk into the hall. Paul rings the bell and Mum dashes out of the kitchen, carrying Maxi. She is whistling. Happy, happy. She opens the door.

"Paul, hi, how did you get on?"

"Yeah, OK, I think," he says. "Last thing I needed today but thanks so much for helping out." He nods to Jay. "Your boots are in the car. We can go soon."

Pops comes downstairs. He has slept late today. His hair is a little wild.

"You up for a game, Spinney?" he says, joining us. His shirt buttons are in the wrong holes. His collar is sticking up like a broken bird wing.

"Pops, this is Jay," I say. "Remember?"

"Yes, of course," says Pops, smiling. "But I can call him Spinney, can't I?"

Mum switches Maxi on to the other hip. He reaches out and Mum can't quite hold him. All his baby strength is pulling towards Paul. He kind of falls into Paul's chest and covers him in snotty, porridgy dribble.

Jay smiles and says, "I-I…" But he can't get the words out.

"Cat got your tongue, young Spinney?" says Pops. "Spit it out!"

Jay turns a bit pink but he also looks at me and I make a face to say I'm really sorry and he just smiles at me and kind of shrugs as if to say, '*It doesn't matter,*' and it feels kind of cool. Like we are really friends now.

He glances at Paul. I think he's worried that Paul heard what Pops said. We both are. But thanks to Maxi, Paul heard nothing. He and Mum are busy wiping the porridgy sludge from his shirt and tie.

"So sorry," says Mum. "Silly thing."

"Game, young Jay?" Pops asks again.

"I can't right now," says Jay. "I-I've got football and I'm at a friend's house later but I'd love to play tomorrow."

"Good-o," says Pops. He looks at Paul. "You've got slobber all down your suit."

Jay and I both smile. We want to laugh. It's so hard not to.

Paul glances down at his tie, brushes his sleeve and turns to Mum. "Could I possibly ask you another big favour?"

"Of course," says Mum, pulling Maxi in tight.

But then Pops shouts, quite loudly.

"That move, Jay, yesterday," he says. "I've remembered. It's called a 'float'. You don't need a build for it."

"Ah," says Jay. "That makes sense. It kind of floats in."

"Yes," says Pops, beaming at Jay. "That's it, it does! Bright lad, your young one here." He points at Paul. "You should be very proud."

Paul nods. "I am."

Pops smiles and then he catches himself in the mirror. He sees his collar like a bird wing and he walks over and starts undoing all his shirt buttons.

Paul looks at his watch and turns back to Mum. "The gas engineers are coming at ten. But I have to get Jay to football and then I must go to the office. Could you possibly meet them and just make sure they know where the gas supply is?"

"Of course!" says Mum.

"Could I show you now? I can just point from the door. You won't have to go in."

"No worries," says Mum.

"Thanks," says Paul. "Come on, Jay. You can wait in the car." He puts his hand on Jay's shoulder and they walk back to their house, Jay waving goodbye.

"Help Pops, will you, Ames?" Mum says, passing me Maxi. She lowers her voice. "It's fantastic that he remembered so much about the game yesterday."

"Why shouldn't I remember?" says Pops, staring at himself in the mirror. "I played that game before I even *met* your mother. I'm hardly going to forget it, am I? And stop fussing. I don't need help. It's just buttons. Everyone thinks I need help these days for everything." He has undone all the buttons and is starting to take off the shirt.

Mum tries to stop him but he shrugs her off. She looks over the road. Paul is waiting.

"Won't be long," she says and she makes a signal to ask me to help Pops and runs over the road.

"Pops," I say. "Keep the shirt on. You were just fixing the buttons, remember?"

"Of course I remember. I remember lots of things."

"Yep," I say. "You do."

I sing to Maxi and pull the shirt on to Pops' shoulder, brushing the cotton as if I've seen a piece of fluff on it. Pops stares at himself and then he looks down and starts doing up the buttons, one by one.

"I forget *some* things, Amy. I do know that. Just like your gran. Old age you know."

It takes a while to do all the buttons. Maxi and I sing

'Wheels on the Bus' several times. Pops looks out of the hall window.

"Who's that your mum's talking to?" he says.

I look out. "That's Paul. He lives in that house."

Pops nods. "With Spinney."

"No, with Jay, Pops."

He stares at me for a second and then he walks away to the kitchen, the back of his shirt sticking out of his trousers. I watch him go and then there is a knock on the door. I know it's definitely Mum because she knocks and rings the bell lots and knocks again. I open the door. She is beaming at me, breathless from rushing.

"You are never going to believe it!" she says, taking Maxi.

"What?" I say. "What?"

"Well, it's the best news. You are going to be *so* pleased with me!"

"OK, what is it?"

She comes in and we close the door. She is excited but for some reason I'm nervous.

"Well, Paul said that if the gas has to be switched off today it's quite good timing because he's away with work tonight and Jay is staying with his friend Josh."

My nerves prickle. I feel a little sick.

"So," Mum carries on, her eyes wide, "I said, oh, is that

Josh as in the Bennett twins? He said yes and, well, to cut a long story short, Paul is going to take you and Jay over for the sleepover tonight and then Cassie's mum is going to run you back tomorrow morning after she's dropped the lads at football. I've just spoken to her." She takes her mobile out of her back pocket and waves it in the air. "It's all sorted. Isn't that the best news?"

I stare at her. It's all sorted. I'm going to Cassie's house with Jay.

"Well?" she says, beaming at me.

I can't move. I just stare at her. She puts Maxi down on the floor and he shuffles across the hall.

"Don't you need me here?" I say. I'm not really in the mood to see Cassie. And an hour in Paul's car. That's a long time.

"No," says Mum, lifting one hand as if there's no need for me to worry. "It's all fine. I'm here. And you and Jay know each other now so I thought it would all work well."

"Yeah, but Maxi needs so much too." I point at him about to lift himself up to standing on the hall table as support. Two picture frames hover and wobble.

"Oh, Amy, you made such a great fuss about missing the sleepover and I've sorted it."

"You could have asked me first, that's all," I say, peeling Maxi away.

Mum stares at me and puts her hands in the air as if she gives up and then we hear a clattering in the kitchen and something smash and Mum stomps off.

Twenty-two

I go back upstairs and lie on my camp bed and stare at the ceiling. My scabies start to race. Why couldn't Mum have asked me? I don't really want to go tonight. I can just see Cassie's face when Jay and I arrive together. She'll be unbearable. I want to just wait for Molly's party in ten days' time.

But it's done and there's nothing I can do. And then my phone beeps.

Cassie.

> OMG just heard ur coming
> with Jay! How come???

> **He's living across the street with his dad**

> OOoooohhh!!! That's great but it's
> a long car journey so don't have
> beans for lunch! 😬 😬 😬

Don't have beans for lunch.

I throw my phone down. Cassie can be *so* annoying.

A few years ago, I had a lift with her and Josh. We were coming home from school. Josh was in the front seat. I was in the back with Cassie and I had wind. It came from nowhere and it was only a very small sound and Josh didn't hear and neither did their mum. But Cassie did. And when the car stopped and the engine was off, Cassie said very loudly, "Sorry if it smells a bit in here. Wasn't me."

I'm not sure Josh or his mum heard. If they did, they ignored Cassie. But Cassie has *never* forgotten and she uses it like a little tool in her toolkit. It comes out just when she needs it. Like when Pops taps through his chisels. The way he taps through them and finds the right one, that's how Cassie chooses the things she says. *Tap, tap, tap*, until she finds the one she needs.

♣ ♣ ♣

It's not long before Mum calls me down. I've calmed down a bit. Molly and I texted about tonight. It will be good to see her.

"The gas people are at Paul's," says Mum. "Will you come with me? Maxi's in a grump. I can't leave him here. Gran's physiotherapist has just arrived."

She picks Maxi up and shoves him under one arm, his

legs kicking out behind him.

We charge over the road. The gas people look up and see us. Maxi is full-out screeching now, arms and legs flailing.

"Someone's not happy," says the gas lady. She leans down and smiles at Maxi. "Can't be that bad." He screams even louder, dribble hanging from his nose and mouth like some sort of alien being.

Mum tells them all the information they need and gives them the key.

"We'll open the door," says the gasman. "You guys, please wait over there." He points to the hedge by the next house and then they both go inside.

Mum and I walk over to the hedge. It's a warm, sunny spot and Mum rocks Maxi, pointing at Jay's cat. It's sitting on the fence. "The cat's not meant to be out," she says. "They've not had him long. But obviously with the gas problem, Paul had to open all the windows and put him in the garden. He did say if we saw him, to try and catch him."

"He looks fine. Hey, Captain!" I make a squeaking sound to get his attention.

"Oh, it's Captain, is it?" says Mum, smiling at me, batting away Maxi's grappling hands pulling at her hair. She gives me this *so you are making new friends that are going to*

Thornberry look. I knew this would happen.

I make a face at her.

"Don't be like that," she says. She hitches Maxi up. "We'll have to try and tempt him down and take him back to ours." We both stare at Captain. He looks away and cleans his fur. "Really could do without this right now. Amy, can you get the tuna from our fridge?"

The gas people come in and out, getting things from the van. I go and get the tuna but when I come back with it and we hold it out, Captain just stares at us. Maxi giggles. Captain has cheered him up. And then Maxi screeches and Captain jumps down and runs into the next-door garden.

Mum says a very bad word.

"Dad won't be happy you said that," I say.

"Well, Dad's not here right now, is he?"

She sounds tired. And cross.

The gas people come out to say they've made everything safe and that Paul needs a new oven and we can go back inside later and close the windows.

We call Captain's name, wander down the side path of the next-door house, tapping the saucer of tuna.

And then our front door opens and Sam yells that Pops is trying to make a cup of tea and we scuttle over the road and when we get to the front door and look back, Captain is up on the fence again, staring at us.

Twenty-three

"We'll be super quick," says Mum, looking at her watch. "It's just after three. Maxi will wake up soon."

We stand on Jay's drive and call Captain's name. Nothing. Mum puts the key in the door and we go inside. The house smells of bleach and polish. Everything in the house is white and clean and sort of empty. It's so different to Gran and Pops' rammed museum and our house with its peeling walls. One of Paul's suits is on the back of the chair in a plastic wrapper. I think Paul likes the house like this. It suits him, all smart and shiny and briefcasey.

"You'd think he'd just moved in," says Mum, shutting the hall window.

"Who?" I say. "Paul or Captain?"

Mum laughs. "I suppose Captain *has* just moved in. I wonder if he's back already. He could have come through a window. Let's see if we can find him."

We go through to the kitchen. There are framed

photographs on the wall. All of Jay. One school photo with no front teeth. One of him with Paul. They are sitting on rocks, fishing. A couple of Jay in football kit. Mum starts to close the kitchen windows and then Captain jumps in through the one over the sink, a flash of black-and-white fur.

"Catch him!" shouts Mum. "He's meant to stay in the kitchen."

Captain darts away. Mum says a bad word.

"You banned that one," I say. "Five-pound fine, you told Dad."

We follow Captain up the stairs.

"There he is!" shouts Mum. "Just saw his tail. Shut all the other doors!"

I shut them all and follow Mum. Into Jay's bedroom.

"He's under the bed," whispers Mum, as if Captain can hear. "We'll have to coax him out." She starts looking around the room for something to use.

I look out of the window, across the road. My bedroom window is right opposite. I can see the net and the peach curtain and a glimpse of a few of the encyclopedia books, lined up on the top shelf. It's like I'm spying on both me and Jay, at the same time.

Jay's bed is in the corner of the room. His duvet is red, the Liverpool logo right in the middle. And there's a penguin tucked by his pillow. The penguin surprises me. I don't know why. There are Liverpool posters all over the wall and one giant poster of the Houston Astros team. I can't work out what sport they play but I'm pretty sure it's in America. They all have shiny white teeth and are wearing caps and padding. There's a signed photo beside it of someone called George Springer, wearing the same kit. A guitar is propped in the corner, next to the bed. There's a basketball hoop and some small foam balls. Socks and T-shirts are scattered across the carpet. Jay has a few books by his bed. *Football Genius. Unbelievable Football. Marcus Rashford: You Are a Champion. Steven Gerrard: My Story.* And then the pile changes. *Stuttering: It's What You Think. Stuttering Help.*

"Should we really be up here?" I feel bad being here. In Jay's room. I wouldn't want someone in mine. Seeing my private things.

"We're hardly burglars, Amy. We can't leave the cat here," she says. "He might go to the loo and cat pee really stinks. He has a litter tray downstairs." She grabs a hockey stick from the pile of things by Jay's window. "I'm going to use this to gently coax him out."

"Let's be quick," I say.

Mum lies down and runs the stick under the bed. "Oh blimey, he's right at the back. Amy, are you listening?" I'm not. I'm staring at the photos on the wall. There's a framed one of Jay's football team and one of him and who I guess is his mum on a boat. And then one with a big wooden sign on the top. It says 'Cousins'. And then I feel a little bit sick.

Mum mumbles something about dust. I grunt a sort of reply.

"Right, I'll drive him out," says Mum. "When I shout, you try to catch him. OK?"

I'm still staring at the photo.

"Come on, pussy cat, come on, Captain," says Mum, very gently. "Nearly got him."

The hockey stick glides out and then slides back in again.

"Amy!" shrieks Mum. She shuffles backwards, bashes her head on the bed frame, says another bad word. "Catch him!" Captain darts out from under the bed and flies out of the door. Mum gets to her knees, expecting me to be holding him. Her hair is a twisted mess, like she's been dragged through cobwebs.

"He went that way," I say, pointing.

Mum sighs. She takes off her hair band and ties it back up. "I really don't have time for this," she says and she storms off. "Come on."

I look back at the photo. There are three cousins. Jay, an older teenage lad and a girl. The girl is staring at the camera, a very faint smile on her face, her hair falling in two straight curtains. It's Dana.

I follow Mum, shut Jay's door behind me, tiptoe down the stairs. Bits of guilt and dread are racing around me like they are two little different types of scabies, bumping into each other as they zip through me.

Captain is in the kitchen, sitting by his bowl. Mum opens a sachet of cat food and feeds him and shuts the door. "We're never getting a cat," she says.

The house feels really cold now, crystal white and clean. Mum is wittering on about the cat and the keys and the gas-leak paperwork but I'm spinning a little. My tummy feels twisty. It's like Dana has crawled out of dance class and crept into this nice new part of my life.

"Come on," says Mum. "Let's go."

We lock up and cross the road. We can hear Maxi screaming. Sam opens the door.

"Look what I found!" he says, holding up a tiny nut.

"In a minute, Sam," says Mum and she runs upstairs to get Maxi. I follow her, race up to my bedroom and go to the window and look back at Jay's. I don't know why I'm doing this. It feels like we've left something or done something wrong. I can just see the edge of one of his posters on the wall. I stare at the window for ages.

When I come back down, Sam is sitting on the bottom stair, his head in his arms.

"What's wrong with you?" I ask, nudging past him.

"No one cares." He blurts it out, looks up briefly and then buries his head again. "I've found this great thing and no one has time to look. Dad always has time to look."

I sit down beside him. Put my head down, just like he's doing. He nudges me, irritated but trying not to smile. We sit for a minute and then I whisper that I want to see and he shows me the nut.

"See these smooth circular holes?" He points to the shell. "It's a dormouse. This is a hazel nut and it's been nibbled by a dormouse." He leans in to me, our knees touching. "There's one right here, Ames, right here in the garden. My best chance is to get it at night. It'll be hard. But they are nocturnal."

"It's good we got Jay's cat back in the house then," I say. "We wouldn't want him catching it."

Sam turns to me, his face horrified. "That can't happen!" he says and he leaves for the garden and I think of Jay's bedroom and the books and the big penguin and the photo of Dana. And how cameras catch moments. And how Mum left the hockey stick poking out from under the bed.

Twenty-four

"So good of your mum to sort out the gas engineers," says Paul.

"No problem," I say. I don't want to add that we played chase with Captain round the house or that I made Mum go back and put the hockey stick away or that I know Jay has a big, cuddly penguin on his bed.

"I was so pleased," says Paul, "that we could help return the favour by taking you with Jay tonight."

"Yes, thanks," I say.

I'm in the back of the car, tucked in a corner, Paul's golf clubs sticking into my thigh. The briefcase is nowhere to be seen. I think it must be locked in the boot.

The car is hot, really hot.

We drive away, Mum waving from the doorstep as if I'm six years old. I think she regretted her wondrous arrangement when Paul backed his big shiny car off the drive. The tyres skidded and Paul beeped the horn really loud. Mum chewed her lip and made a signal to call her. She'll worry until I say I'm there.

"Wait, we have to go back," says Jay, patting all his pockets. "Now! Go back, I've forgotten my ear pods. Dad, turn round."

"I can't. I'm late already. You'll just have to cope."

"I need them," says Jay. He spins round and stares at Paul as if Paul is refusing to go back for essential, life-saving medication. "I *can't* not have them." The car stops at the traffic lights.

Paul sighs. I think if I wasn't here, squashed next to the golf clubs, this argument would be bigger. He looks at me in the rear-view mirror. "Amy, I don't suppose you have a spare pair?"

"Um, no, sorry," I say. I want to laugh. Please, don't let me laugh. I can just see Jay wearing my old ear pods, twisting the wire to try and make the sound work.

The lights turn green. Jay slumps down in his seat. The back of his neck shows through the headrest. He makes a noise. It reminds me of the sounds the cows made on holiday, when they were being led to the milking shed. It's funny seeing Jay like this but then I think of how mad I get, how my scabies start to race round me and I wonder if that's how Jay feels right now. Just like he felt this morning when his dad tried to make him phone Cassie's mum.

Maybe the ear pods really help. Maybe it means he doesn't need to talk as much.

"Are your friends going tonight, Amy?" asks Paul.

"Um, yeah," I say.

And then Paul's phone rings and he says, "Sorry, I need to get this," and he presses a button on the screen and a lady's voice booms through the car. Mum would not like this. Even though she does it.

I watch the houses flash by and then the green fields as we wind through the lanes. I think of Molly walking round to Cassie's house, all so easy, and I wish I could still do that too.

Paul keeps talking.

"That software is too expensive... I'll go to the conference..." There are lots of words I don't understand.

My phone beeps. It's Mum, asking if everything is OK and did I pack my night things. I double check. Everything is there. I feel a bit nervous again, about the sleepover. It feels like I'm holding on to that rope again but it's greasy and I'm slipping, all my friends on one side, me on the other. But I'm not alone now. I'm with Dana. And she is ignoring me and then laughing when I fall.

Paul's call ends. The golf club with the big round end is really hurting my thigh. Whenever Paul turns round a corner, the whole bag slips further towards me. I think my thigh might have a dent in it forever. But even moving seems too noisy right now. So I stay still. Just try and nudge the bag back a little.

Paul flicks on the radio and the music is so loud that it wouldn't matter *too* much if I had wind, because no one would hear. And then because I've thought about it, I want to have wind so I have to sit up a little and twist.

Paul stops to get petrol. He is right by my window, filling up the engine. And then he goes into the shop to pay and he has to wait at the back of a long queue.

The car is very quiet. I wish Jay had his ear pods in because I'm still thinking I might have wind. I'm so worried that the silence now is like a big balloon that's been blown to full stretch and my wind would make it go pop.

"Are you staying over?" I say. Of course, I know he is. I just want the quiet to not be such a big thing.

"What?" he says, turning his head slightly. His face still looks a bit grumpy, from the ear pod thing.

I feel silly having said anything. I just felt I should. And then I feel mean for making Jay talk. Me and my stupid mouth again.

"Um, are you staying over? You know, at Cassie and Josh's tonight?" I reach for my bag and put it on my lap, as if we've arrived and I'm ready to get out.

"Yep, we're camping in the garden." He stops and turns round slightly and tries to smile, as if he's just realized he was still looking moody before. I want to tell him that I have grumpy moods that don't go quickly. It's totally fine. "I-I hate sleeping in a tent," he says.

"Oh, me too," I say. "I'm on a camp bed right now and it's the most uncomfortable thing. It collapses most nights."

Jay nods and smiles. It feels easier now, chatting in the car. I wonder if I should ask about Dana, tell Jay that I know her, find out if he sees her much. But then Paul comes back, and throws a tube of sweets at each of us.

"Thanks," I say.

Jay grunts a bit. He unwraps one and puts it in his mouth. And then he throws himself forward and spits it straight out.

"Oh my God!" he yells. "I hate liquorice. You know that."

Paul has started the engine but he gets out of the car and grabs blue tissue from the pully thing next to the petrol pump. He comes back and shoves it at Jay.

"Pick it up and put it in the bin."

"I don't want to get out," hisses Jay, as if he doesn't want me to hear. "I'll do it later. You know I hate those sweets."

I think Jay has the scabies again. I feel bad being here. I wouldn't want anyone to see me when my scabies are racing.

"Now," says Paul. "Or I don't move." He turns the engine off.

I sink deeper into my seat. The golf club sinks deeper into my thigh.

We sit like that for a bit. The car is very quiet again. Jay stares out of the window at the pump. I wonder if he has a book on being stubborn. *Stubbornness: Your Survival Guide*. And then the car behind beeps its horn. It wants to go. Jay snatches the blue paper and bends down to pick up the spat-out sweet. And then he gets out and puts it in the bin and charges back to the car.

Paul drives away, the tyres squealing a bit. We get back on the main road and then Paul holds up the packet of rejected sweets.

"Why don't you have these, Amy, as I made such a bad choice?"

"Um," I say. "OK." I'm not sure which way I should go here. Maybe if I take it, I'll be like one of those peace-keeping people, sent to break up problems.

"She won't like them," mutters Jay. Paul glares at him.

"Oh, I do, I do," I say and I reach for the packet. "They're actually my total favourites. Let's swap." I pass forward the lovely little tube of unopened pastilles. Jay takes them and then glances back at me and holds them up and makes a puzzled face as if he knows I like pastilles so why would I swap?

Paul looks at me in the mirror.

"You would say, wouldn't you, Amy, if you didn't like them?"

"Yeah!" I say. I lift the liquorice packet up so Paul can see me take the next sweet. I put it in my mouth and chew the revolting liquorice. I bury the tube deep in my bag, never to be seen again.

And then I have to twist and squirm a lot and it's not just because my mouth is full of revolting liquorice but because I really can feel a bit of wind coming on. Maybe there's a book called *Farting HELP*. I'd buy it for sure.

Twenty-five

We pull up at Cassie's house. Her dad, Gareth, is on the drive, washing his car. He waves and smiles, soapy suds dripping from his hand.

Paul waves back and turns off the engine. "So you know the plan?" he says, turning to face Jay. "Josh's mum is taking you both to football in the morning and I'm getting you at the end of the day. You have your kit, yes?"

Jay holds up his bag. "Yep."

"Sorry about the ear pods, mate," says Paul. He lowers his voice but I just hear. "I know they help."

"It's OK," says Jay.

"Blimey," says Paul. "That liquorice was strong! Your tongue is black."

Jay pulls down the sun-visor thing and looks in the mirror.

"Great," he says in a sarcastic voice. He clicks off his seat belt. "Can we get Chinese tomorrow?"

"Absolutely," says Paul. It's funny then because after all the irritable stuff Paul and Jay just sit for a moment. And then Paul leans over to Jay and Jay leans over to him and they do this little fist-bump thing.

I feel a bit silly sitting in the back with the golf clubs watching them. I wonder if I'll have to fist-bump Paul. Maybe Paul fist-bumps everyone. I don't even know *how* to fist-bump.

Jay gets out. Paul yells at Gareth through the open door.

"Thanks, mate!" They wave and then Jay shuts the door and I open mine.

"Have fun, Amy," says Paul. OK great. No fist-bumping.

"Thanks," I say and I climb out. Before he sets off I put my tongue out and catch my reflection in the glass. It's black.

Paul beeps the horn and pulls away. We stand for a second. Jay gets his towel out of his bag and rubs his tongue. I find a tissue and do the same to mine.

"Is it bad?" he says and he sticks out his tongue.

"It's pretty black," I say. "Mine is too."

He looks at the house and sighs. "She'll have fun with this," he says, quietly so Gareth can't hear.

"Who?" I say.

And then the front door opens and Cassie shrieks, "They're here!" She looks behind her and yells, "Everyone, come and see! Jay and Cassie have arrived – TOGETHER!"

"Who else?" says Jay. He says Hi to Gareth and then goes straight into the house, head down, ignoring Cassie.

I walk slowly up the path, wiping my tongue against the top of my mouth, thinking about what Jay said.

"Hey, Amy," says Gareth, sponging the soapy liquid over the wheels. I lift one hand and wave. I want to grab the sponge and scrub my tongue.

I get to the front door.

"Good journey?" says Cassie, nudging me.

I ignore her.

Molly gives me a hug. "So glad you're here," she says. Her gorgeous dark hair brushes my cheek and she smells of peaches. She always does.

Cassie's mum Nicky joins us.

"Hey, Amy love. Your mum just called to see if you were here. Will you text her?" I nod. "Are you hungry?" she says.

I shake my head and say, "I'm fine thanks."

"Oh my God!" shrieks Cassie, pointing. "Your tongue is jet black!" She grabs her phone from her pocket and tries to take a photo.

I want to call Mum and tell her to ask Paul to turn round and get me. I'll just cover myself in golf clubs and disappear. Jay was right. Cassie is going to have fun with this.

"Come and put your things upstairs," says Molly, waving Cassie's phone away and grabbing my hand.

But then the boys race past us, Jay sticking his tongue out like a zombie, Amil and Josh laughing and chasing after him.

"Whoa!" says Cassie. "Jay's tongue is black *too*!" She screeches, as if this is just too much fun. "What *have* you two been doing in the car?" She follows the boys out on to the drive, snapping away on her phone.

"I need the loo," I say and I run up the stairs and into the bathroom. I'm so mad with Cassie. She doesn't think about who she's hurting. I bet she starts something about me fancying Jay. Just like she started something about me having scabies. I stick my tongue out and try to rub the black away but it won't budge.

Molly knocks on the door. "You OK?"

"Yep," I call. "Coming."

I join her on the landing. "Ignore her," she says. We go into Cassie's room. Her mum has laid out three beds in a row, all with duvets.

Cassie bursts in. "We're going to have a competition – see who can get the blackest tongue! Where are the sweets? Jay says you have them."

I'm *really* happy to give them to Cassie. If we *all* have

black tongues, that will hopefully make the whole thing go away.

I tip my bag out. She grabs the sweets and leaves.

My phone starts ringing from inside the zipped pocket in my bag. I get it out. It's Mum.

"Hi," I say. "I'm here." Molly gives a little wave and goes downstairs. I sit down on Cassie's bed. Her new school blazer is hanging on the wardrobe handle. The Valley High emblem is golden on the pocket.

"Oh!" says Mum. "Thank goodness for that."

"Yep." I force back a tear. I'm back in my old village. My old house is just round the corner, the house I love. Jasmine is probably in my bedroom, right now, looking at the clouds on the ceiling, watching the evening sunlight dance on the wall.

"You OK, love?" says Mum. I bite my lip, walk to the window. Jay and Josh are sitting on the bench drinking Coke, chatting. Amil is lining up shooting targets in goal.

I don't know if I'm OK. I've loved the jigsaws and shove ha'penny and being with everyone at Gran and Pops' house. It's been nice getting to know Jay. But now our new friendship is mixing in with my old life and it seems odd. Like someone's stirred sauce on to your ice cream and you're not sure if it's made it better or not.

I'd forgotten about the big problem for a few days. That I've got to follow a completely different path. But it's right back now at the front of my mind, all around me in Cassie's house.

I want to tell Mum that I don't feel great. I'm not sure I want to stay. But then Maxi cries out and I can hear Pops. And I know I might cry. So I just say, "I'm fine. Gotta go. Bye."

"OK, love," says Mum. "Have fun!" and she hangs up.

I watch Cassie in the garden. She's passing round the sweets, trying to make Molly and the boys take one. I don't think they want to. Only Josh eats his. Cassie shoves three in her mouth and then yells for them all to see.

Twenty-six

The boys have a tepee tent in the garden. Nicky has put a lantern in it and laid out beds for them. They have a big bucket of sweets, just like us. I can see it from where I'm sitting, round the firepit.

Me and Molly watch Cassie in goal, leaping from side to side, arguing with Josh about whether the ball went over the line. She is hot and sweaty and she doesn't care. I like that about Cassie.

"It was definitely a goal!" says Amil.

"Jay!" yells Josh. "What do you think?" He looks at Jay. Jay stares at him, looks down, bounces the ball. I don't think he can find the words. But Josh waits.

"I saved it, idiot!" shouts Cassie at her brother.

Josh scowls at her and waits. He knows to wait. I'm glad Jay has a friend like that.

"I-I'd say it went over," says Jay.

"Yeah, right," says Cassie and she gets ready to face the

next ball.

Josh and Jay hand-slap.

"Is it fun being at your gran's?" asks Molly.

"Kind of," I say. "Hopefully she'll be well enough to take care of Pops again soon."

"Why, is he ill?" says Molly.

I shrug and say, "No," but then I start to cry. I didn't think I was going to. But it just sort of grabs me. So I tell Molly. About Pops and his memory problems and the scampi lunch and my flat bed. Molly is a very good listener. I tell her about shove ha'penny and Spinney. And I tell her about Jay and the gas leak and chasing his cat and the drive in the car.

But I don't tell her that me and Mum went in Jay's room or about his books on helping him not to stutter or about the photo of Dana. I want to close that part of the day in my mind. Like I wish his bedroom door had been closed and we had chased Captain out of another room.

"So do you think your thigh will recover?" she says, giggling. "Or will you always have the golf-ball dent?"

"I think it's set in for*ever*!" I laugh.

Cassie joins us, wiping her sweaty hair off her face.

"What's funny?" she says.

"Nothing," I say. I don't want to tell Cassie. She will tell everyone. She'll probably announce a 'golf-club-thigh-dent competition'.

"Why can't you tell me?" she says.

"It's nothing," says Molly.

"Well, if it's nothing, why can't you tell me?"

She glares at us. I go to say something but then I can't think what to say. She'll know I've made something up. Cassie has this way of knowing.

"Were you talking about me?" she says.

"No, Cass," sighs Molly. "It was nothing about you."

"Then tell me."

Gareth comes in the back gate of the garden. He's carrying a huge pile of take-out pizza boxes.

"Anyone hungry?" he shouts. "Veggie, pepperoni and margherita. Two of each." The boys stop playing football and run over.

My phone beeps from my pocket. I take it out. Mum has sent a photo of Gran, dressed up as a mouse. She has her grey hat on with two big ears stuck in the wool and whiskers drawn on her face. She is in front of the trap cam, posing. I can just see Sam at the side, laughing so hard he is clutching his sides. I burst into giggles.

"What is it?" says Molly. I pass the phone over.

"Show me," says Cassie. She goes to grab the phone but

Molly turns a little, trying to see for herself first.

"Come and get them!" shouts Gareth.

"Show me," says Cassie again, but Molly is enlarging the photo, trying to make it out.

Cassie turns away, folds her arms. She's annoyed. She thinks we're hiding something from her. She walks over to her dad and goes to take a box.

"Wait!" says Gareth, looking at the order list taped to the boxes. "I think this is Molly's. She's got extra mushrooms. Jay, which one did you order?"

He looks up at Jay.

Nothing comes.

I watch him. Jay tries to speak. He looks down, shifts a little. I know the signs now.

Molly elbows me. She realizes what the photo is. She sees Gran is a mouse. She grabs me and says, "Your gran is *mad!*"

"Completely!" I say, and I look over again at the phone, both of us laughing.

At the same time, Cassie says, "They'll be stone cold if we have to wait any longer."

Jay spins round and looks at us. He thinks we're laughing at what Cassie said. My laugh snaps away. No one else heard what Cassie said. Just me and Jay. Amil and Josh were chasing after the ball. Cassie's dad was studying the order list. Molly was too busy looking at the photo.

I look at Jay. I point at my phone to show him what we were laughing at. He turns away and says, "Pepperoni," and reaches for a pizza box.

Cassie turns back to us. "Molly, are you veggie with extra mushrooms?" She just doesn't care. She's said this horrible thing and she doesn't care at all.

Molly jumps up. "Yep!" she says. "Come on!" She grabs my arm. We collect our boxes and take them back to the fire.

I lift the lid of the box but I can't eat a thing. I stare at the circle of bread and cheese and pepperoni. Jay was so honest with me this morning. It's like I've taken that and stamped on it. I'd hate him to think I would find *anything* like that funny.

"Oh my God, this is the best pizza," says Molly, strings of cheese dangling from her mouth. The others eat and I stare at the fire, picking at the crust. My tummy feels like concrete. The boys are sitting on the grass. Jay has his back to me. He's laughing and chatting and I hope, really hope, he knows the truth.

Gareth comes over.

"Everyone happy?" he says. We all say yes and I lift a slice and bite it and try to eat.

Twenty-seven

The boys have gone inside. We can see them through the glass doors, gaming. They all have headphones on and they are madly pressing the controls.

"I'm going to play with them in a bit," says Cassie. "I always beat Josh at FIFA. He's rubbish."

Molly picks up a stick and pokes the fire. We have a few more marshmallows to toast. She passes me one and I slide it on the skewer.

"So," says Cassie, elbowing me gently. "Have you seen Jay every day then?"

"Um, sort of," I say.

"I knew he was at his dad's house all week."

Molly looks at me and rolls her eyes as if to say, '*Here she goes again.*'

"He comes to our house *all* the time," says Cassie. "Part of our family really."

"Oh," I say.

It's like Cassie is jealous I'm friends with Jay. Nice one minute, cruel the next, as if she can't work out which one to choose. Like her mind is a jungle of paths and she's never sure which one she's on.

"Y-yes, he i-is," she says, a smirk on her face. And then she spurts out her Diet Coke, all over her lap.

I look back at the house, to check they're all still gaming and that Jay didn't hear. "I can't believe you just did that." I pull the marshmallow out of the fire.

"Yeah," says Molly. "Not funny at all."

"Oh, I'm only messing," says Cassie. "I'd never say anything to him."

"You did earlier," I say.

"When?"

"You said the pizza would go cold if we waited for Jay to speak." I look back again to the house.

"Did you?" says Molly. "That's not very nice."

"I didn't!" says Cassie.

I glare at her. "You said 'they'll be stone cold if we wait.'"

"It was just a joke," says Cassie. "You guys take everything so *seriously*." She flicks her hair back and digs her heels into the grass, pushing at the turf so it scuffs up. "He's Josh's best mate. He's always round here. We're always messing about. Anyway, he's over it mostly now. He's had that speech therapy thing. It was loads worse a few years ago. He told Josh that."

I feel a bit odd, us talking about Jay like this. He might not want us to know that. Cassie can never keep anything to herself.

"It doesn't mean you poke fun," says Molly quietly.

Cassie rocks her head from side to side, mimicking Molly.

"Sometimes," I say, staring at her, "you say things that are horrid and I hate it when you do that." I take a little breath. I've never said that to Cassie before.

She gets up and walks away, throwing her pizza box into the fire. The flames lick round it and Molly uses her stick to push it properly on. We watch Cassie go back into the house, arms folded, head down.

"Wow," says Molly. "Well done."

We sit close together, staring at the fire.

After a few minutes, there is a screech from the house. Cassie is trying to get the control off Josh. He is fighting back, pulling it away. Cassie's parents go in and sort it out. There's more shouting and then a minute later Cassie is back out with us, mumbling and grumbling, slumped by the fire, her head buried in between her knees.

It feels good, Cassie not getting her way. Cassie being told she's wrong.

I lift the lid of my pizza box and take a slice. It's a bit cold but I'm hungry now and the stodgy cheese tastes amazing.

❧ ❧ ❧

We have the best ice creams for dessert. They are covered in chunky chocolate.

Cassie holds hers by the fire. It's dying now but there's enough warmth to just melt the chocolate. It runs down her fingers.

"What food will we have at your party?" she asks Molly.

"Just pizza, I think."

"But we've had pizza tonight," says Cassie. "Why don't you do sushi? Or Tex-Mex? Remember that great Tex-Mex food at my party last year?"

"No," says Molly.

"You had chicken wraps at your party last year, Cass," I say.

"Yeah, Tex-Mex," she says. "Tex-Mex wraps." They weren't Tex-Mex. But I can't be bothered to argue again.

"Mum's making this mocktail thing," says Molly. "She's bought a kit. You can make all sorts of cool drinks in champagne glasses. And we're getting nail polish and tattoos. Do you think that sounds OK?"

"Sounds amazing," I say.

"Who's coming?" says Cassie. She leans over and throws her lolly stick in the fire.

"Everyone," says Molly. She glances at me and makes a worried face, biting her lip. That means Jess is coming.

"Who's everyone?" says Cassie.

Molly takes a big bite of her ice cream. I can tell she doesn't want to talk about it. She bites a bit hard and grimaces.

"Why are you making that face?" says Cassie.

"It was the ice cream," says Molly. "It was super cold."

"I know it was about me and Jess and our fallout. It was her fault! She sent me that really mean message when I'd been honest about the necklace breaking."

Molly and I don't say a thing. We just stare at the fire.

"She did," says Cassie. "You don't believe me, do you?"

Molly chews on her stick and I pick up bits of small twigs and throw them in the flames. It's hard with Cassie and Jess. There's always *something* going on with them.

"Well," says Cassie. "I don't care anyway. And if everyone is coming then it doesn't matter, does it? There'll be tons of us there. The boys must be coming too."

"No," says Molly. "I haven't asked them."

"Well, then I'll go and ask them now." She stands up and goes back inside.

"Cass, no!" I say but it's no use.

"What's with her tonight?" says Molly.

We watch Cassie through the window in the den, talking to the boys. They're all on the sofa, staring at the TV, headphones on. Cassie is behind them. She babbles away and points outside.

"I don't think they can hear her," I say.

They carry on gaming, each desperately pressing buttons. Cassie talks away, pointing again at Molly. She smiles at us, as if pleased we are witnessing it all.

"You're right," says Molly. "They can't."

We turn back to the firepit and it's so hard not to collapse into giggles but we know Cassie will be mad if she sees. So we just clutch each other and chew on our ice-cream sticks.

"I can't believe she did that!" I say, when we've calmed down.

"I can," says Molly.

We look back again. Josh has passed Cassie his control and she's settling down to play the game. She's pointing at the screen, yelling instructions. I can just see the tip of her black tongue.

"I hope Jess and Cassie will be OK," I say.

"They'll have to be," says Molly. "Cassie was so stupid. You don't borrow a friend's favourite necklace and then take it apart to make it shorter."

"I know. I don't think she meant to be that stupid," I say.

Molly sighs.

"I don't think she ever means to be..."

Josh comes out and joins us, taking a marshmallow from the packet and sticking it on a skewer.

I sit back and watch the fire.

Cassie borrowed Jess's necklace to go to her aunty's wedding. It was too long to match her dress and in a panic she put a knot in it to make it shorter. Two of the beads broke away and rolled off, right under the posh chairs. She searched after the service and even went back the next day with her mum to see if they could find them. But the beads were lost and Jess was mad.

Jess gets mad very easily.

And Cassie does stupid things very easily.

Twenty-eight

Nicky has a big, old, rattly car. The good thing about the big car with its deep, squidgy seats is that if you're in the back, the front seems very far away. Cassie is in the front and she seems far away and that's good because I've had enough of Cassie right now.

"You guys look knackered!" says Nicky. She looks at me in the mirror. "The boys struggled to get up too. They had to be at football by nine!"

"Yuck," says Cassie.

"Did you get *any* sleep?" She glances at Cassie and then me in the mirror.

Cassie shrugs and I say, "A bit," and I smile at her mum.

The radio is on. Nicky turns it up and I sit back and look out of the window. We pass our old road. The tree with yellow flowers flashes by. I can almost see my old house where Jasmine now lives. I turn away. I can't bear seeing it.

Cassie spins round and holds up her phone. It's a photo of the lads with black tongues. I nod and give her the tiniest smile and then look out of the window again as if I'm truly engrossed in the local shops. We turn on to the main road and go past the turning for our new house. I think of Dad working hard and I wish I could see him. I send him a text to tell him I miss him and then I stick in my ear pods, wiggle the wire to make them work and close my eyes. I think of Jay, doing the same thing to escape.

At last, we pull up at Gran and Pops'.

"I'll just come and say hi," says Nicky. "Haven't seen your mum for ages."

We get out and walk up the path and Cassie elbows me.

"Where does Jay live?"

I point over the road. Captain is sitting in the front window.

"Cute cat," says Cassie.

"Mmm," I say. I think of last night again, how Jay must have thought we were laughing at what Cassie said and my tummy aches. Just that one thought has made me feel sick, as if I will not be able to eat a thing all day.

Sam opens the door. He's holding the trap cam.

"You will *not* believe this!" he says.

"Not now," I say. "Where's Mum?" But he has stomped

off and after a few seconds I hear *Tom and Jerry* blasting from the lounge.

Mum comes out of the kitchen carrying Maxi. Cassie reaches for him and he happily sticks out his gooey hand. "Can I take him?" she asks and Mum passes him over.

"There's a basket of toys in the front room," she says and Cassie takes him to find them. I go upstairs and put my bag in my room. When I come out, I see Sam sitting on Mum's bed, looking at the trap cam. He has muddy knees and sticky-up hair. I remember how homesick I felt that morning and how much I wanted to see Dad. Sam must be feeling that too.

"Come on then," I say, plonking down next to him. "What you got?"

He presses a few buttons.

"It's a fox. It's so beautiful!" He presses the buttons and I watch the short piece of film. The fox comes close to the camera, almost looks down the lens. Then it turns and the last thing you see is its bushy tail.

"I'm happy for you, Sammy," I say. "Dad will love to see it." I give him a fond nudge and go downstairs.

Cassie is making a tower with the big wooden blocks. She makes the tower really tall and then Maxi knocks it down and screeches and Cassie smiles and I think how quickly Cassie can change. She's like that cartoon Mum showed me that was on years ago. This guy goes into a room and comes out as a different character. Knight, astronaut, clown. That's a bit like Cassie. Like she has a magic room. And lots of outfits.

Cassie keeps stacking the blocks but she says, "I'll see you next Saturday, won't I?"

"Yeah," I say. "I'll be there."

She tucks her hair behind her ear, pulls Maxi on to her lap with a book.

"Do you think Jess will be OK with me?"

"Yeah," I say.

"Mum and I got the necklace fixed and we've tried to buy a new one but they don't sell them any more." She turns the page and makes the sound of a roaring lion.

"Have you told Jess that?" I say.

"Yeah," says Cassie. "Look, Maxi, a monkey!"

"It will be fine," I say.

Cassie makes a monkey sound and Maxi copies her, a line of dribble rolling down his chin.

"Did you have fun last night?" she asks, looking up at me, eyes wide, keen to hear the right answer.

I stare at her. I want to tell her I'm still annoyed about her teasing Jay but it doesn't feel the right time.

"Yeah, course," I say, tidying Maxi's books into a pile.

"I didn't really invite the boys. To Moll's. I was just pretending. They had their headphones on. And I'm sure Jay didn't hear me, you know, when I was being silly."

Cassie always does this. Like she knows she hasn't been very nice and that she needs to make up for it before she goes.

"I think he did," I say.

She spins round to look at me.

"Oh," she says. She looks a little lost, worried. I don't see Cassie like this very often. She strokes Maxi's hair, hugs him a little. "I hope he didn't."

I think of how Jay saw us laughing and how awful I felt.

"I think he did," I say again. She looks at me and doesn't say anything, just hugs Maxi and turns the page, quacking quietly like a duck.

Her mum comes in.

"We're off, Cass," she says.

Cassie passes Maxi to me and we both walk out to the front doorstep. She looks over at Jay's house. She's about to say something but she stops herself and then she just says, "The cat's gone."

They walk down the drive and get in the car and pull away, Cassie waving from the window with a little smile.

I have that feeling I always have when I've been with Cassie. Like you've been to the beach and it was cold and rained a lot but in the last hour the sun came out and gave you little glimpses of how good it can be.

Twenty-nine

The cottage door is the hardest bit. The pieces are all the same colour, just a few knots of the wood setting them apart.

"Nearly there," says Pops. He fits the last three pieces into the doorway. "We did it!" he shouts. I get up and walk round to his chair and I wrap my arms around him.

"Let's show everyone, Pops, like we always do. Gran won't believe we've done it so quickly!" He pats my hand and then he leans forward, looks at the picture and slowly swipes the whole jigsaw on to the floor.

We both stare at the pieces. The sky is shattered, a pile of blue and orange and pink. The cottage is broken but the door is there, every piece of it, all the knots of wood lined up perfectly. I don't let go of Pops but all I think of is the cartoon man and the door he goes through and how he changes every time.

"We can do it again another day, Pops," I say and he nods. He gets up slowly from the table and walks to his big armchair in the corner. He sits down and closes his eyes. I bend down and reach for the box and start putting the pieces away. I lift the door whole. The pieces are tight and I lay the door on the top of the box, as if it's ready to be opened.

And then I kiss Pops on his cheek and leave quickly because I don't want him to see that I'm about to cry.

♣ ♣ ♣

I've been asleep for hours. After lunch, I snuggled next to the boys to watch cartoons. Maxi went up for a nap so I sneaked off to bed too and caught up after the sleepover. I've given up putting the bed on its legs. It just lies flat on the floor. Mum gave me an extra duvet to pad it out and it's not too bad now.

I look at my phone.

Dad has texted.

> How was the sleepover? Doing great here.
> That wallpaper you despise is in the skip!
> Shall I keep a square of it for you? 😆

I message back.

> **Sleepover was good. No thanks –
> never want to see that wallpaper
> again!!! Miss u xxx**

There's a message from Molly too.

Great 2 see u! Can't wait for the party
next weekend! 😺

I send her a line of heart emojis.

I hear a car outside. It's Paul and Jay. I duck behind the curtain and watch. Jay gets out. He's in his football kit. Paul goes to the boot and gets out his briefcase. Captain is at the window again. Jay walks over and taps on the glass and Captain stands up and lifts his nose.

Paul walks to the front door, searching in his pockets. He doesn't have a key. I think in all the gas drama they've locked themselves out. He looks at our house and realizes Mum has the spare key. I pull right back from the curtain. He's talking to Jay. He's pointing at our house. I bet he wants Jay to come over and ask for it. One of his little 'tasks'. Jay looks over the road. He's shaking his head and saying no. And then I have a funny feeling in my tummy. He doesn't want to come over. Doesn't want to see me again. If he thought we were laughing at him last night, why would he?

Paul walks over the road and knocks loudly on the door. I hear Mum whistling, walking towards the front door. And then muffled voices and laughter. Mum calls up the stairs.

"Amy love, could you come down for a sec?"

I don't want to go downstairs. Jay must think I am the most horrible person.

I go to the door and do a sort of whisper-shout down to Mum.

"Why?"

"Paul needs the spare key but I can't remember where on *earth* I put it. Do you remember?"

"Don't know," I say. "Sorry."

"Can you come and help me look?" And then I hear her tell Paul that she'll just check in the kitchen.

I go back into my room and look outside again. Jay is shooting hoops on his drive. I go to the landing, hover for a minute hoping Mum'll find it. She's on her way back. I look down. She has Gran's cake tin full of the terrible cakes I made. I dart back to the doorway of my room.

"Do have one of these," she says. "Amy made them." And then I hear her shout Jay's name, asking him to come for cake. And then she raises her voice and I can tell she means for me to hear. "Amy is coming right *now* to help me."

I lean against the door. This is going to be so awkward. I breathe deeply and go downstairs and sit on the bottom step.

"Ooh, yes," says Mum. "You might need to come in if I can't find it. Maybe boots off, Jay. Thanks."

Paul is standing in the hall. Jay is behind him, bending down to take off his boots. Mum puts the cake tin down and moves the things on the table in the hall, searching for the key, opening drawers. Paul is holding two of my rock cakes, his briefcase clamped in between his feet as if it holds something *really* important. Like the code to a room of gadgets.

"Great," says Mum, looking at me. "You're here."

"Hi," I say.

Jay looks up just for a second and lifts one hand in a wave. And then he bends back down to his boots. He must be pleased to have a reason not to talk to me.

It's all a bit icky. We really need to find the key.

"Thanks so much for helping yesterday again, by the way," says Paul.

"Oh, any time," says Mum, rustling through the drawer in the hall. "I hope it's sorted now. We couldn't smell a thing when we came to check on things, you know, check on the cat, find the cat." She closes the drawer, wipes her hands on her apron. She's in a right fluster. "The cat got out. So then we went back to get him in. And he ran upstairs."

"I'm sorry it took up so much of your time," says Paul.

Jay's boots are off. He stands up and Paul passes him a cake and he peels the case off, picking at the crumbs.

"We wanted to check he was safe," says Mum. "He's speedy, isn't he? He ran under Jay's bed and we couldn't get him out at first, could we, Amy?"

Thanks, Mum. That's great. Now Jay knows we were in his room. He's already super mad at me and now he knows we've been in his room.

"Um ... no," I say. "You sorted it really, Mum, didn't you?" I tuck myself against the banister.

"I had to use your hockey stick, Jay," says Mum. "I hope that was OK? Of course, we didn't hit the cat. Just coaxed him. Ever so gently."

Oh my God, Mum, you're making it worse and worse.

"And then you know what?" she says, shaking a pile of envelopes in the hope a key will fall out. "We got home and realized we'd left the hockey stick poking out."

Oh God. My cheeks are on fire.

"Amy was most insistent I go back and put the stick back so that no one thought we'd been sneaking round in your room, Jay. What a thing."

I'm staring at my feet. Every part of me is hot.

"But we got Captain out in the end," says Mum, tipping the hats from the basket by the front door. "And we didn't pee anywhere, um, no, I mean the *cat* didn't pee anywhere and all is fine, yes?"

Paul nods. "I really appreciate it. I'm sorry Captain was such a pain."

"No worries at all!" says Mum. "Happy to help." She thrusts her hands in her apron pocket and tips back on her heels and then she laughs and stops.

"What do you know?" She pulls out the key and says, "Here it is!" and she passes it over.

Paul takes it. Everyone is a little relieved. You can feel it in the air. Like a cool breeze blowing in.

Gran joins us. She leans one crutch against the wall and picks up the tin of cakes.

"Do have another," she says. But they haven't choked down the first one yet.

Jay passes his cake to Paul and bends down to put his boots back on again.

"And I have to say, Jay," says Mum. Oh blimey. She's off again. "You and Amy share something." Oh no. Please no. "She loves penguins too, don't you, Ames?"

I literally can't believe she just said that. I glare at her.

Jay now knows that I know he has a big, cuddly penguin on his pillow.

I look at Jay. He looks at me. And then I just say, "I do."

"Big time!" says Mum.

I'm going to be sick. Or hot flames will pop out of my ears. Right now. One of the two.

"Ah, the penguin!" says Paul. "It was a souvenir from a

party Jay had at the zoo for his birthday. Good few years back now, hey, Jay?"

Jay grunts and ties his boots tight.

"Oh, how wonderful," says Mum. "Would you recommend it? Sam would love that."

Jay stands up and nods and says, "Definitely."

"He's special, that penguin," says Paul. "Isn't he, Jay?"

Jay nods and half flicks his face round, smiles a little.

"Yep," he says. I can just see Jay's right cheek, blushed pink. No wonder. We've just completely embarrassed him. I'm dying too. Me and Jay just slowly crumbling inside. He already hates me after last night and the pizza thing and now he thinks we've been snooping round his room. He takes the cake back and picks at it, eats a bit.

"Do you remember, Susan?" says Paul. Gran looks at him and then down at the path, thinking. "The penguin at the window?"

"Oh, of course!" says Gran. "Oh, that was *so* lovely!"

Jay looks at me and makes a really funny eyebrow-raised face as if to say, '*Here he goes.*' I smile back, all of me feeling a bit better. He can't be *really* mad if he's made a look like that.

"When Pattie and I first split up," says Paul, "I moved out and worked nights. I didn't have my own place for a bit so Jay stayed with Pattie most of the time and he'd put the

193

penguin in the window each night with different outfits or sunglasses. It would be just for me to see, on the way home."

Jay nods and smiles and folds the cake case into a tiny ball.

"When we came to live here, he did it a few times didn't he, Susan, you saw it! Just a few times when he had a sitter and I was late back."

"Yes," laughs Gran. "And I passed the penguin back one day, when he fell out of the window on to the grass and you hadn't seen him!"

Paul wraps an arm around Jay and hugs him.

"Yeah, we'd had a bit of a tiff," says Paul. "Remember? Think he might have been pushed that time!"

Jay laughs. "He jumped! He's a stunt penguin."

Everyone laughs. I can imagine it happening. Paul and Jay having an argument and then making up with a fist-bump.

Paul picks up his briefcase, spare key in his other hand, ready to go.

And then Pops pads out from the front room. He has taken his slippers off and his big toe is sticking out of a hole in his sock.

"Is that Spinney?"

Jay raises a hand.

"Hey, you coming for a game, young Jay? If that's OK with your dad? Me, you and Amy. Quick go on the board?" Pops' face is so bright, his eyes keen. Jay looks down, is quiet. I'm not sure if he can't find the words or he doesn't want to be here, with me. Maybe he's still a bit upset deep down.

I start to speak, to tell Pops that I'll play with him but then Jay says, "Would that be OK?" He's looking at his dad. He actually looks pleased.

"Please don't worry," says Mum. "I'm sure you're busy. Dad just loved getting the board out again."

"Oh, he *really* did!" says Gran.

"No, it's fine," says Paul. "I've ordered the Chinese for seven but that's a while away yet, so how about Jay has a quick shower and then heads over?"

"Let's set it up in the lounge," says Mum. "We can clear the sideboard. What do you think?"

"Good plan," says Pops. "I'll get the board right now."

Jay and Paul leave, it's all sorted.

Pops turns to go to his shed.

"Slippers on, Dad!" calls Mum.

"Or shoes would be even better," adds Gran.

Pops turns back and stares at them. It's as if he has no idea what they're talking about. His face is blank, his eyes a little glazed.

"I'm getting the board for Spinney," he says and he turns and walks away in his socks, softly chanting, "*The board, the board, Spinney, come quick, you'll never be bored with a board to unpick.*"

Gran passes me the tin and closes the door, takes a breath, hobbles after Pops.

I open the tin and try a cake. It's not too bad. I look back through the little hall window. Paul is opening the front door. Jay is taking his boots off again. I take another bite, get a chocolate chip this time.

I like the penguin story.

I *still* have to say something about the laughing thing last night.

I think about what Cassie said and how Jay saw us laugh and the cake turns into a stodgy ball in my mouth and I spit out what's left, into the paper case.

Thirty

Jay knocks on the door. I look at the clock. It's six. We have an hour. I open the door. He's changed into jeans with a rip on the knees and a sports top. It's got ASTROS written on the front.

"Dad sent these," says Jay. He has a huge bag of sweets. "No liquorice!" We both smile. I close the front door.

"Pops is talcing up the board," I say.

He offers me a sweet.

I take one from the bag, start unwrapping the paper. I need to say something before we start playing or I might not get the chance. My mouth is very dry.

"Um … did you like the pizza?" I ask. "The pizza last night."

He nods, rummages in the bag for another. I take a deep breath.

"What Cassie said – when the pizza was being given out – Molly and I didn't like it." He picks out a sweet and puts it in his mouth. "We told her we didn't like it."

He looks at me and raises his eyebrows, makes a funny smile as if we were brave to tell her.

"We were laughing," I say. "But not at that."

He looks at me and says, "No worries."

"We were laughing at this." I get my phone from my pocket. "It's Gran, dressed up as a mouse!" He stares at it, enlarges it, smiles. I'm worried now that the photo doesn't look funny enough to have made us laugh so much. Jay passes my phone back. Offers me another sweet.

"I just wanted to tell you," I say. "That's all."

"It doesn't matter," he says. The relief pours through me. I chew on the sweet. Jay offers me another. "I can't even remember what she said. She says things like that all the time."

"Oh."

"I-I don't know why. To get laughs probably."

"Well," I say. "It wasn't funny and I told her so."

"Thanks," says Jay.

I nod. The lounge door opens.

"Come on, you two," calls Pops. "We're all set up."

I feel so much better. As if I was covered in mud and I've stood in a hot shower and washed it all away.

The large sideboard has been cleared of all the photos

and trinkets and vases. There is a cloth under the board and the lip is hooked on the edge. It's a good height.

Jay offers Pops a sweet.

"Don't tell the dragon!" says Pops, taking one and nodding towards the kitchen.

"Pops!" I shout. "Do you mean Gran?"

"I sure do. Dragon. I'm not allowed many sweets these days." He smiles and picks up the coins. "She hides the biscuits. I know she does. OK, who's going first?"

We play for ages. Jay wins one. Pops wins two. I don't win any. Pops smiles the whole time. It's like he's checking into the past. He's back in the pub, with Spinney.

"You should play this at school!" says Pops. Neither of us say anything. "You're going to the same high school, is that right?"

I turn to Pops and smile. He's remembered something I told him yesterday. He usually forgets new things.

"Yep," says Jay. I don't say anything. I don't want to get into the whole high school saga right now.

"Are you nervous?" asks Pops.

Jay shrugs. "A bit."

"I expect you are," says Pops. He leans down to take his go, lining up the coin on the edge of the board. "Probably a bit more than most, with your stutter."

I freeze. Stare at Jay. But he just nods. He doesn't mind at all that Pops has mentioned it.

"I see something very fine in you," says Pops. "Be yourself, always." He flicks the coin, knocks his other coin into the lane so it sits exactly where it's meant to be, takes the chalk and puts a third mark in the box.

Jay laughs. "Good move!" he says.

"Spinney had a lot to deal with in life," says Pops. "But he always used to say, '*Be yourself. Stay strong. Always see the silver lining.*' That was Spinney for you."

"Where's Spinney now?" I ask.

Pops stares at me and says, "Now? Right now? I don't know."

"Did you keep in touch?" I ask.

"For a while we did," says Pops. "And then he moved away. America, I think. Gosh, I wonder where he is now."

"I bet we could find him," says Jay. "If you wanted to. My dad's good at that stuff."

Pops looks at Jay.

"Really? Find Spinney?" He looks away, stares down at the coin in his hand. "When was that?"

I'm not sure Pops knows if we are talking about now, then, yesterday, the future or the past. I'm realizing that time for Pops is like Maxi's golden spinning top. It twists and spins and then you wait and wait for it to settle. I think Pops waits a lot for it to settle. But sometimes it just keeps spinning.

"Your go again, Pops," I say. He takes the coin, turns it gently and carefully glides his coin down the second lane. It's like Pops has spun back in. The coin sits in the lane.

"A perfect float," says Jay and Pops turns and winks at him and chalks up the score.

Jay lines up his coins ready.

Pops turns one of the coins in his hand, looks out of the window and says very gently, "*Spinney, you marvel, you win every time. Spinney, you marvel, let the coins float in line.*"

Thirty-one

"I miss Dad," I say, leaning down to rest my head on Mum's shoulder. She's at the kitchen table, working on her laptop.

"I know," says Mum. "So do I. But he's doing so well with the house. He's going to send more photos later."

I sit down and pick up a sheet of paper covered in numbers.

"How do you understand all this stuff?" I say.

She laughs. "I don't always."

Sam comes in. He's ready for bed. He wraps himself around Mum. "When are we seeing Dad?" he says.

"Soon," says Mum, packing up the papers. "And you'll never believe it. The giant skip that was on the drive is full already! A new one is coming tomorrow."

"They better not move that bug house I made," says Sam. Mum looks at me so he can't see and makes a funny face as if she knows the bug house has already gone.

Sam gets a cup and opens the fridge to find the milk. "I'm

watching that nature programme with Pops. Did you know Pops and Gran went to Kenya on safari? I'm so jealous." He wonders off, his dressing-gown belt dragging along the floor.

Mum turns to me and closes her laptop.

"I'm nearly done," she says. "I just need to talk to you about something." She strokes my cheek, pulls me into her. "I spoke to the schools department at the council this morning. We're now fifth in line. But they did say that as the weeks go by it's more unlikely places will come up." She's talking gently, as if she's giving me bad news, as if I'm about to hear which tooth is to be pulled out.

I'm very still, just staring at the columns of numbers on the top of the pile.

"I also phoned Thornberry this morning. The receptionist was so helpful. Your form tutor has agreed to come in on Monday to meet us, which I thought was fantastic. We can have a look round. Dad can come too. It's still the plan to go to Valley High but it's looking more and more…" She stops there and neatens the pile of paper.

"Unlikely," I say.

She nods.

"I don't have much choice, do I?"

She shakes her head.

I want to say, 'But you promised.'

We promise, Amy, that if we move, we will make sure you go to Valley High with your friends.

But then Mum says, "We made a mistake, Ames. We made a mistake saying that we would definitely get you into Valley High. Dad and I are very, very sorry about that."

The house is quiet. The cuckoo clock chimes in the lounge. A car revs outside. Gran's crutches tap on her wooden bedroom floor.

Pops and Sam laugh loudly. It rattles through the house. Gran calls down from upstairs, "Do be quiet, you'll wake Maxi," and Pops shouts back, "Be quiet yourself then, Dragon."

Mum winces. And then Gran calls down, "I'll start breathing fire on you soon, old man."

We both smile and I don't say anything about Valley High or Thornberry or promises. I just hug her and stare at the numbers, trying to make sense of all the columns.

Thirty-two

Mum's cooked scrambled eggs and bacon and toast for breakfast.

"We're going out for the day," she says. She's emptying the dishwasher, stacking the plates in a pile. "Pops insists and I think I've found a solution. He woke up rambling on and on about the baboons on that nature programme last night. He's determined to go to the zoo. But it would be too busy. He'd hate it. And Gran can't walk around a zoo right now. But I had a brilliant idea!"

"What is it?" I say. I'm not liking this. Mum's last brilliant idea was to stick me in Paul's car for an hour with a big, round club thumping into my leg.

"A day out at the safari park!" she says, beaming at me. "They have baboons there and we just drive around. We can put the extra seats up in the back of the car to make it a seven-seater. You and Sam can sit in those…" She says it quickly, hoping I haven't fully heard that bit but I throw

205

my head back and silently screech. I hate those seats. You have to squash yourself in. They're fine for bringing five of my friends back from the cinema, or for Sam and his friend Alfie to sit in and wave at other drivers. But a whole day at the safari park ... this will be worse than the golf clubs.

Mum is still talking, rattling away while she's cutting sandwiches in half. "Pops can sit next to Maxi. I'll make sure the child locks are firmly in place so he can't open the door. It's perfect. Change of scene for us all and no one needs to get out."

"Where is Pops?" I hiss. I'd hate him to hear that. About the child locks.

"He's in the lounge, looking for information on baboons. He's convinced they brought a guidebook back from Kenya." She bends down, looking for some tupperware. "You're the last one down for brekkie," she says. "So eat up and we can get going."

I think of sitting in the car all day, in that tiny seat, like a toddler. I'm not in the mood for the safari. I want to just stay here. Do the jigsaw again, maybe play shove ha'penny. See Jay when he's home. Get ready for Monday and visiting Thornberry.

My scabies stir. They jolt awake. I try and squash them. I know I'm being unfair but they won't listen.

"If we can all go to the safari," I say, scraping my chair back, "then on Wednesday night, why couldn't you have driven me to the sleepover and put Pops in the back with the child lock on?" I slam my glass of juice down, fold my arms. "You never think about these things when it's just about me."

Mum stares at me hard. I flick my eyes up at her. She has scrambled egg in her hair. The toast pops up and she reaches for it and plonks it on my plate. "We leave at ten," she says, her voice snappy and sharp. "I've booked it, I've paid for it. I've made a picnic for it." And then she leaves the room.

I sit down and bite into the toast and make a face to mimic her. I pull the fat off the bacon and get a serviette to wipe my hands. Mum has put out special breakfast serviettes, each one folded in two, the used ones crumpled up on plates. There are flowers in a little vase. Maybe she hoped we would all sit round the table singing, '*We're going to the zoo, zoo, zoo…*' I scoop up some eggs. Mum makes the best scrambled eggs.

Pops wanders in.

"I found it!" he says. "*The Masai Mara Mammals: Your Safari Guide.*" He holds the guidebook up. "It was olive baboons we saw." He flicks through the pages and shows me.

"We might see them today, Pops," I say.

He shakes his head. "Not round these parts. You don't

get baboons and lions roaming round here, love."

"I know, Pops, but we're going to the safari park, aren't we? All of us in the car."

"Where?" he says, staring at me, and then he pads away and I notice his slippers are on the wrong feet.

I pile up the plates and feel bad for being grumpy with Mum. I stack the dishwasher and wipe the surfaces. I make a fresh bottle of squash and find some crisps and clean serviettes to take with us.

Mum comes back in. She's had a shower and put some make-up on. I wrap myself around her and she hugs me back tight and we stand for a few seconds just like that and she smells so good.

"Sorry," I whisper.

"It's OK," she says, rocking me a little. "I'll buy you a souvenir at the safari park. Maybe a baboon fridge magnet."

"Wow, my friends will be *so* jealous," I say and we stand there a little longer, laughing, wrapped together tight.

Thirty-three

We drive up to the entrance. Mum shows the tickets on her phone. She's a bit flustered because it took ages to get out of the house. Pops didn't want to come. He sat in his chair, clutching the paper, saying that he didn't really feel like going to Kenya today.

"I need the toilet," says Pops.

Gran turns quickly to Mum and then looks round to Pops.

"You sure, love?" she says.

"Of course I'm sure," he says. "Why would I say that if I didn't?"

Mum leans out of the window and speaks to the girl at the counter.

"Where are the toilets, please?" She lowers her voice, "And is there a disabled one?"

The girl points and we drive off, across a large paved area towards a line of concrete buildings.

"Why do we need a disabled one?" says Pops.

We are all quiet.

"Yeah," says Sam. "Why does Pops need a disabled one? That's crazy!"

I shove him hard. He hits me. I grab his wrist.

"Stop it!" yells Mum.

"It's for me," shouts Gran to the back of the car. "With my ankle and crutches. I need the bigger space."

"Oh," says Sam. "Why didn't you just say?"

Mum reaches across and holds Gran's hand.

We park and Mum gets out and opens Pops' door.

"I'll go first!" says Gran and she hobbles out of the car and limps towards the disabled toilet. Mum waits with Pops, talking to him all the time, showing the map of the safari park, pointing to the baboons' enclosure. I think she's worried that Pops will see the men's toilet block and decide to just go in there. Which he can't. We all know that now, after the pub.

Gran is quick. I'm not sure she even went. She wants to go in with Pops but he won't let her. So they have to jam something in the doorway so he doesn't lock it. There's a bit of an argument about that. Sam and I peep through the gaps in the back seat, trying to work out what they're saying. Maxi laughs at us, as if we're in one of those booths at the seaside you stick your face in to have a photo taken.

"I hate seeing Pops like this," says Sam.

"I know," I say. Maxi gets a clump of my hair and pulls it. I yelp and have to grab his sticky, chubby fingers and peel the strands free.

After a while, Pops comes out. Gran sprays his hands with sanitizer and they all climb back in the car.

It feels like the whole world has come here today. We're sitting in a long train of cars, the sun bouncing off the metal roofs. We trundle over cattle grids and into the park. Maxi twists and squirms in his seat. Pops stares out of the window at the grass and the meadows and then up to the sky.

"The sky today, Amy," he says, twisting his head to the side and up to try and see as much sky as possible, "is like the jigsaw."

"It is," I say. "Same sort of scattered clouds."

"Yes," says Pops. "Spinney would like these clouds. Always find the silver lining, he'd say." He is very still and quiet, staring up. "Every cloud has one."

Sam has got Mum's phone and is taking photos. The antelope and camels, the rhino way in the distance.

"That's a white rhino," he says, pointing. "Did you know their name has nothing to do with being white?"

"No," says Mum. "Tell us."

"Well," says Sam, "it comes from the Afrikaans word 'weit' which means wide, used for the rhino because of its *wide* mouth. People think it's to do with the colour white but it's not."

OK, so that's fairly interesting.

"How do you know all these things, Sam?" asks Gran.

"I just do," says Sam. "That was in my wildlife magazine."

We drive through a set of gates and into a different grassed area. An enormous cow is grazing.

"Look," I say, "on my side. They don't look like they should be in a safari park."

Sam squeezes over and looks out of my window.

"You say that," he says. "But that's a European bison. Numbers are recovering but they're endangered. They were wiped out in the wild once."

"Has Maxi seen it?" says Mum, glancing in her mirror. "He loves cows. Oh blimey. He's fast asleep." And then she laughs. "And so is Gran!"

"Where are the cheetahs?" says Pops.

"No cheetahs here," says Mum. "But we're going to see the baboons soon, Dad. And the lions and elephants."

"Oh," says Pops. "I wanted to see the cheetahs. We saw one, Suzie, on that safari in Kenya. Do you remember?"

"Mum's asleep, Dad," says Mum.

Pops tuts. "Again?" he says. "She could sleep all day, that one."

"No," mutters Gran. "I'm not asleep. Just resting my eyes. What was that?"

"The cheetahs, Mum, on your safari," says Mum. "Do you remember them?"

"Of course," says Gran. "We spent every day in the Masai Mara searching for them, didn't we, love?"

"It was the last day, wasn't it, Suzie?" says Pops. "You spotted it first, right in the distance."

Gran turns round and squeezes Pops' knee. "I did," she says.

"Do you have photos?" I ask. "Of the trip."

"Gosh," says Gran. "Somewhere, in an album."

"I'd love to see them."

Sam rustles the map.

"Look, Chinese water deer. They have little fangs." We all look round to watch them. One looks up startled. I get my phone out and take a photo. They are super cute.

The sign comes up for the baboons. There are two routes. The car-friendly one outside the enclosure and one that goes right through it.

"Shall we drive through?" says Mum. "The monkeys can climb on the car."

"Of course, we must," says Pops. "Sam will like that, won't you, Sam?"

Sam shrugs. "I think so," he says. "If the baboons like it."

Mum drives through the big, metal gates. "Can't believe I'm going to say this," she says. "But wake Maxi up."

I lean forward and prod him and shake him a little but he's fast asleep. We drive on. The car in front is covered in little baboons, chasing across the roof. And then one leaps straight on to the bonnet of our car. Another jumps up, right near Maxi's window. There's a lot of monkey noise, deep grunts that build to loud, piercing shrieks. Maxi wakes up. He's staring straight into the face of a baboon. He screeches and the baboon runs away.

Maxi bursts into tears.

"You're fine, Maxi," says Mum, turning round and smiling at him. "Monkeys!" she says and she makes a monkey sound.

Another one jumps on the front bonnet and a smaller one joins it. Mum stops the car.

"I'm not sure about this now," she says. Sam and I look at each other, both of us wide-eyed and smiling.

"Bit like being in a movie," says Gran, with a nervous laugh. "It feels like a giant T-Rex might stamp past in a minute."

Maxi stops crying and watches the baboons, laughing as

they itch their tummies and stare through the windscreen. Pops tries to open his door.

"We can't get out, Pops," I say. "We're not allowed."

"Oh," he says. "You can get out at the zoo."

One of the baboons lifts the windscreen wiper and shakes it like it's a toy.

"I'm really not sure about this," says Mum.

But then Maxi starts giggling, really giggling, like he's being tickled and then Pops starts laughing and Sam and I join in and the car is full of laughter. The bigger baboon pushes the other one and the two of them fight over the wiper. The smaller one twists round and his bright red bottom is pressing on the glass. Maxi is almost breathless he is laughing so much. Pops slaps his leg with the joy of it and Gran has to get a tissue to wipe her eyes.

A big gap has opened up before the next car.

"We need to move on," says Mum. She drives on slowly and the monkeys jump off.

"That was amazing," says Sam. "I got loads of photos to send to Dad!"

"Let's hope the wipers are OK," says Mum, testing them out. "Everyone all right?" She glances at us in the mirror, looks for me. I smile and nod and she wrinkles her nose and smiles a little at me as if to say, '*It was fun, wasn't it.*'

We drive out of the enclosure, all of us turning and twisting to watch the baboons as they race on to the cars behind.

"Gosh," says Gran. "I haven't laughed like that for ages."

"The sky is so blue," says Pops. I can just see the side of his face. It has changed. It's very still. He looks out of the window and I do too. The sun is beaming, the sky hot and blue with just a few scattered wisps of white.

We drive out of the enclosure, through the big, metal gates. There are green fields around us again and a buffalo is grazing by the side of the road.

"I'd like to go home now," says Pops.

Gran passes him a sandwich.

"I didn't ask for a sandwich," he says.

"Thought you might like it, love."

He throws it on the floor. No one says anything.

Maxi starts squirming in his seat. Gran passes him a pot of Cheerios. He bashes it away and they fly across the car.

"Worse than the monkey house," laughs Mum but her voice doesn't sound so happy. The fun of the moment has gone, snapped away. She grips the steering wheel a little tighter and glances at Pops in the mirror. But then Gran says, "I'll always remember this trip." Mum grabs her hand and nods and I say, "Totally." And Sam says, "It was wicked."

I reach forward and pass Maxi his comfort blanket and his drinking cup. He settles and quietens down.

I look down at the map.

"Just the lions left, Pops," I say. "Then home."

"I like lions," says Pops. "I'd like a sandwich." Gran passes another back to him and he bites it. Mum drives on, spraying the windscreen to check the wipers are working properly. I think of home and I realize that for the first time I think of home as the musty, mouldy new house and I really can't wait to see Dad and all his hard work.

Thirty-four

It takes a long time to drive back. Maxi falls asleep, his giraffe tucked under his chin.

"Great trip," says Gran as Mum pulls on to the drive. "Nice cup of tea now."

Pops tries to open the car door.

"It's locked," I say, holding his arm. "To keep Maxi safe."

"Oh," says Pops. "Is that Maxi?" He points to him.

"Yep," says Mum. "You know Maxi. He's your grandson." She jumps out and comes round and opens Pops' door.

"No, he's not!" says Pops, undoing his seat belt. "Sam is my grandson." He gets out and then stops and looks around him, staring at each house.

"You OK, Dad?" says Mum.

He doesn't answer. She takes his arm but he won't move. I think of the spinning top again, whizzing round, waiting to find a place to land. Gran clambers out of the car. Mum pulls the seats forward so that Sam and I can heave ourselves out of the back. We all gather by Pops, waiting.

"Come on, love," says Gran, waving one crutch in the air. "Let's go." She pulls him but he won't move.

"I don't know this house," he says.

"Of course you do," says Gran. "Look, there's the stone hedgehog. We always look out for Spikey, don't we? Every time we come home. And there's Sam's bird feeder that he hung up yesterday." She pulls him again. But he won't move.

Paul's car drives up and he and Jay get out. Pops watches them and then he relaxes, lifts one hand and points.

"Good old Spinney Jay!"

"Yes," says Mum, waving at them. "That's Paul and Jay." I can tell she's relieved. Pops is checking back in, like he's arrived again. Paul waves back and then he jogs across the road to join us.

"Not the best time," whispers Mum.

Jay follows Paul, bouncing his football. His kit is covered in mud. When they reach us, he taps it gently to me and I tap it back.

"Have you finished your footie camp now, Jay?" asks Mum.

He shakes his head. Tries to say something. But he can't.

"No," says Paul.

It's odd but Jay kind of scowls at his dad a bit. I don't think he liked him jumping in.

"Big match against a Manchester team on Sunday," says Paul. "And then Monday to Wednesday training, and then I pass him back to his mum, nice and exhausted!"

"Sounds good," says Mum.

"Have you all been out for the day?" asks Paul.

"To the safari park," says Sam, holding up his map. "The baboons ran all over the car and pulled the windscreen wiper!"

"We haven't been there for years," says Paul. "Do they still have the sea lions?"

"We didn't do that bit," says Mum. "Shame. Next time."

Oh, here we go. Sea lions. Penguins. Mum's off again. I rummage in my pocket and glance at Jay. He's kicking the ball up in the air, over and over.

"We were just wondering," says Paul. "It's Jay's birthday tomorrow. Eleven years old. Can't believe it. Would Amy like to join us for a bit of cake?"

I smile and nod. I'm so pleased the whole pizza thing is forgotten, done with. Jay must have agreed Paul would invite me.

"Jay's mum and some family are coming too," says Paul. "One of Jay's cousins is Amy's age and going to the same high school. Might be nice for them to meet up. Just a bit of cake and piñata bashing at say, two thirty?"

I stare at Paul. Dana will be there. I don't want to go if Dana is there. I don't want to mix knowing Jay and knowing Dana. I can't smile any more. I turn round and reach into the car for my bag.

"Oh, that's wonderful!" says Mum. I turn back and she's beaming at me like I'm six and I've just been chosen to play Mary in the school nativity. "*So* kind of you! And how great, Amy. You can meet someone else going to Thornberry!"

I want to say, '*I don't need to meet the someone else. I've met her. She doesn't like me.*'

But of course, I can't.

Somehow, I manage to talk. My mouth is bone dry. "Are we definitely free?" I say.

"Of course!" says Mum. "You lucky thing! A party!"

She'll be talking about me wearing a pink frilly dress next, with a matching wand and wings.

"It's not really a party," says Jay.

"He didn't want one!" says Paul, nudging Jay. "But I said we had to have cake and a piñata!"

Jay looks at me and raises his eyebrows and rolls his eyes as if to say, '*Can't believe he's making me do this.*'

It makes me smile. I feel a bit better. He taps the football to me again and I tap it back.

Pops leans towards Jay. "You coming for a quick shove ha'penny game, Spinney?"

Jay flicks the ball up so he can catch it. He bounces the ball, flicks his hair, looks up again.

Gran rests her hand on Pops' sleeve. "I'm sure Jay has better things to do than play that ancient, dusty game."

But Jay looks at Pops and says, "I-I'd love a quick game, if that's OK." He looks at Paul who nods.

"This Spinney," says Paul. "He sounds quite the character!"

"Oh, he is!" says Pops. "He went to America. Found a new life. Not seen him for a long, long time." He stops and looks around him. "Have I, Suzie?"

"No, you haven't," says Gran. "We've no idea where he is. America, we think."

Pops nods. "This is our house," he says. "Isn't it?"

"Yes, it is," says Gran.

Paul smiles. It's a little sort of understanding smile. And then he says, "If you ever wanted to find Spinney, I'm pretty good at that sort of thing. I've found cousins for my friend, in Australia. We could give it a go. Sounds like you had great times together."

"Find Jerry Spinneyfields?" says Pops. "That would be unbelievable." He rocks back on his heels and looks up at the sky and then grabs Gran's arm and they clasp hands, tight.

Gran nods and mouths 'thanks' to Paul and then leads Pops up the path, leaning on his arm for support, one crutch tapping on the concrete.

"Have a think about it," says Paul to Mum. "It would be my pleasure to find your dad's friend." He turns to go and then calls back, "I'll send Jay over in a half hour, for a quick game. I'm sure you're all tired after your day out."

Mum waves and we unload the bags from the car. Maxi wakes up, crying and whining. I unclip him and lift him out of his seat. He's covered in food and dribble and spilled drink. He wraps himself around me, his little arms round my neck. I walk up the path and try to ignore all the revolting stuff being squashed against my favourite T-shirt but I really don't mind. It's been a good day after all.

Thirty-five

"Here you go," says Mum. She passes me a large box, wrapped in gold. "That's the best wrapping paper Gran could find."

"What is it?" I ask.

"A ball."

I stare at her.

"*A ball?*" I say it as though a ball is the most bizarre gift in the world to give a footballer. "Please tell me it's a decent one. Not a beach ball or one of those foam balls Maxi has."

"I'm sure Dad ordered a good one. Lucky it arrived in time. Jay will love it." She looks at her watch. "You need to go."

I don't want to go. I don't want to see Dana. My tummy is full of squirmy, nervy worms. But Jay asked me and I can't let him down. It's nice to think he wants me there.

I go over the road and knock on the door and Jay answers.

"Happy birthday," I say. I've got the box tucked under my arm, like you'd carry a school folder or your lunch box.

"Thanks." He lets me in. There is a spread of food on the

kitchen counter and a little pile of presents so I nestle the box in at the back. I follow Jay outside because that's what I think I should do.

"Hey, Amy," says Paul. He's cooking sausages on the barbecue. "This is Pattie, Jay's Mum." Pattie is tall and very beautiful and she is holding a glass of wine like they do on the adverts.

"Hi, Amy," she says. "I've heard so much about you and your lovely family. It's great that you and Jay are going to high school together." I smile and say thanks.

"Do you like sausages?" says Paul.

"Oh yeah," I say. I'm so nervous right now I couldn't even nibble a chipolata.

"Good stuff," says Paul. "Not like missy here." He nods towards Pattie. "Vegan, this one. All very admirable but nothing beats a good sausage, hey, Amy?"

I have no idea what to say.

"Do shut up, Paul." Pattie laughs. "No wonder you and I could never last!"

They laugh a bit and start to talk about plans with Jay this week and I watch them for a moment and think how great it is for Jay that his parents are like this. Sophia's mum and dad split up a few years ago and they can't even be in the same room.

Jay brings me a Coke and asks if I want to shoot some hoops. I say yes but then the doorbell goes, loud and long.

"OK, everyone, hold on tight!" says Pattie. She leans in to me and says, "My sister can be a little bit loud! Hope you brought your ear muffs!" She drifts off to answer the door and I watch her dress billow as she goes.

Jay follows her. I sip my Coke and hover in the doorway. The bell goes again.

"OK, OK!" yells Pattie and she opens the door and there is screaming and shouting and laughing and Dana walks in with the biggest bunch of balloons I've ever seen. Her brother is carrying a giant present. He dumps it on the floor and grabs a handful of crisps from the bowl.

"Now, everyone," says Pattie. "This is Amy, Jay's friend from across the road. And Amy, this is Dana and Tucker and their mum Clare."

I like the way she says I'm Jay's friend.

I *don't* like the way Dana stares at me. She's having a hard time working out what I'm doing here. I'm just the girl she doesn't like at dance with the horrid new top.

I raise a hand in a wave. Her nose wrinkles like it does sometimes. Her hair is in the normal long straight curtains, but on one side is a small, glittery clip.

Clare smiles at me. Jay and Tucker playfight a bit,

wrestling on the kitchen floor.

"Where's the cake?" asks Pattie.

Clare stares at her and then squeals a little and slaps her hand over her mouth.

"I completely forgot to pick it up!" she says. "I'll have to go back for it!"

"I just asked you to do that *one* thing," says Pattie.

"It won't take long, Pats. But the shops will be heaving. It'll be impossible to park. Dana, you come with me and you can jump out and get it. You might need some help, though. I ordered the giant one!"

"Jay can go with you," says Pattie. She spins round to find him but Jay and Tucker are now on the lawn tumbling over each other, screaming with laughter. She calls his name but he doesn't hear.

"I'll have to come," says Pattie. She puts her wine glass down.

And then Clare looks at me and says, "Amy, would you like to come? You and Dana could get to know each other better."

I think I'd rather tumble round the lawn squashed between Jay and Tucker.

I nod a little and move my mouth up at the sides.

"We'll leave these two hulks to fight it out!" says Clare,

nodding at the boys. "Come on!" Dana is standing very still, staring at her nails. She doesn't want me to come. It's obvious.

I follow them out to the drive and get into Dana's mum's car. And then I have a thought. Mum doesn't know I'm doing this. It feels a bit odd. She always knows where I am.

"Sorry," I say. "I just need the loo." And I run back into the house and find the loo downstairs. I get my phone and call Mum and she answers straight away. And then I've got to talk quietly because I don't want anyone else to hear.

"Is it OK if I go with Dana, that girl from dance, and her mum to go and pick up a cake?"

"Is Dana there at Jay's house?" says Mum.

"Yeah," I say, rolling my eyes. "She's Jay's cousin."

"Oh, that's wonderful!" says Mum. "You can get to know each other even *more* before high school. How great! Have fun."

I don't want to know Dana more.

"OK, bye," I say and I hang up and wish I hadn't bothered calling her. And then I pee and try to make sure I haven't got any wind which is easier than I thought because just as I sit down on the toilet Pattie puts on some really loud music and no one will hear any noise I make anyway.

Thirty-six

Clare's car is very small. Tucker must have to squeeze himself in. Dana goes in the front seat. We pull away and Clare puts on some music.

"So," she says, "Dana told me you're both going to Thornberry."

I don't say anything. I want to say, 'No, I'm not. I'm going to Valley High with everyone I know.' But it seems a bit silly to say that now. So I just say, "Yes."

"Are you excited?" says Clare, turning down the radio so she can hear me better.

"Um," I say. "Sort of."

"Good for you. Dana's dreading it a bit aren't you, love?"

Dana spins round and glares at her mum. "I'm not," she says. "All my friends are going. Amy doesn't know *anyone*. Only me."

"Well, you'll have to help her then, Dana, won't you?" She glances at her. "Because you know lots of people."

I'm not sure I want to meet Dana's bunch.

"And Jay," I say. "I know Jay now."

"Great," says Clare. "You were at primary together, is that right?"

"Yeah, and my grandparents live over the road from Paul's house."

"It's funny," says Clare, tapping the steering wheel. "I'm just thinking..."

Oh no, please don't think. Please don't invite me for tea or to the cinema or to meet Dana's friends.

"I'm sure I've seen you before, Amy." She glances at me in the rear-view mirror. "Scouts maybe?"

"Amy goes to street dance," mutters Dana, staring out of the window.

I sit very still and stare at my hands in my lap.

"Oh, now I get it! Of course!" says Clare, slapping the steering wheel. "You're the *famous* Amy from dance!"

I'm frozen now.

The famous Amy.

What has Dana said about me to make Clare say *that*?

Dana turns the volume up and music bursts into the car. Clare turns it down and says, "Oh, Amy, I'm *always* hearing about you! Every Tuesday on the way home!" She glances at me again in the mirror.

"Oh, really?" I say, lifting my eyes briefly. My tummy aches, like I've just swallowed a lump of slime. Dana bends down and rummages in her bag.

"Oh yes!" says her mum. "Super Dance Amy we call you! Dana always says how you get all the moves right and how lovely you are to everyone and a couple of weeks back, she went on and on about a new top you had. Purple, was it? And I had to go *straight* out and find the same one."

I stare at the grey pattern of threads on the headrest.

"I *didn't* say that," says Dana. She glares at her mum.

"Yes, you did, Dana!" Clare laughs out loud and looks at her as if she's surprised Dana is being like this. "I couldn't find it, though," says Clare. "It wasn't on any of the racks in the dance shop."

I wonder if I should say, '*Did you try the bargain bucket? The one by the door where all the unwanted tops with holes go?*' but I don't.

Super Dance Amy.

Total shocker. Dana likes me. So why is she so odd around me? Why does she make me feel the complete opposite?

"OK, here we are," says Clare and it's a relief to get off the dance thing. "It's busy, like I thought." She pulls over by the entrance and we get out. "I'll drive round the car park and come back to meet you. Just give them our name. Thanks, girls!"

She drives away and I follow Dana inside. The shop sells bread and pastries and cakes and it smells amazing. There is a huge mirror behind the counter and the shelves are full of cake tins. There are a few tables where you can sit and eat.

We wait by the till. Dana looks round and then gasps a little and flicks her head back. I turn to look. There's a group of girls in one corner, drinking milkshakes.

"Just my luck," she says. She fumbles with her hair and pulls out the little shiny clip. And then she turns back and waves to them. They don't wave back but just sort of nod. She looks away and turns a bit pink, fiddles with her bag. I can see the girls in the mirror, reflected. They are all heads down now, giggling and waving just like Dana did.

I don't like them.

We wait for ages, creeping slowly forward in the queue. The more we shuffle, the closer we get to the table of girls. I keep looking at the reflection. They are chatting away and laughing at their phones.

Clare drives past outside the shop.

It gets a bit awkward, so I say, "Did you go to the last dance session on Tuesday? I had to miss it."

Dana sniffs and nods and gets a tissue out of her bag.

"Yeah, Jamila did the dance fest. We made up this new routine to some really cool music and had snacks at the end." She blows her nose and flicks her hair back.

"It sounds great," I say. "I'll miss dance over the summer."

She nods and glances at me. "Me too."

"You can have that top if you want. The purple one. I don't like it really. I only have one so Mum bought it for me as a spare."

Dana kind of shakes her head and shrugs. She wipes her nose again and puts the tissue away. We are next in line to be served. But then I notice that Dana has something hanging out of her nostril. It looks like a giant bogey. I don't know if I should say anything. I look round at the girls at the table. They are finishing up, about to go. I lean in to Dana.

"Dana, you have something sticking out of your nose. I'd wipe it if I were you." She flicks round to look at me and then she looks in the mirror behind the counter. There is a gasp and she rustles for her tissue and wipes her nose.

"Oh my God, thanks so much," she says.

The girls walk past us. They ignore Dana.

"They would have never shut up about that, if they'd seen," and then she glances at me and smiles a little.

The lady behind the counter asks us what we would like and Dana gives her the details. The lady goes into the back of the shop and comes out with an enormous white box. I've never seen such a big box for a cake. We take it from her, laughing as we balance it between us. We have to lean forward a bit and Dana's hair falls over her face, the curtains pulling together. We shuffle out of the shop and wait for Clare.

Dana looks at me and then looks away again.

"You're really good at dance," she says.

"So are you," I say.

"I'm not. But I want to get better. The dance studio at Thornberry is amazing."

"I've not seen it yet."

"You've not *seen* it yet?" she says, her eyes wide and surprised.

"I'm going on a tour on Monday. I'm still trying to get into Valley High."

Dana shifts her end of the box and she says, "It must be hard."

I nod and tilt my end and we feel the cake slide a bit and we both shriek and gasp and make it level. Dana looks at me and she smiles and I think it's the first time I've seen her smile in a normal way.

"You should put the hair clip back in," I say. "It's nice."

And then Clare pulls up and we decide the best way to

keep the cake safe is to have it in between us on the back seat, wedged in. We set off. Clare has to brake hard at the lights. The box slides and tips and we both shriek and dive forward and grab the edges just in time to stop it slipping down on to the floor.

"See if you can use the seat belt," says Clare. Dana rummages for the middle belt and pulls it round the front of the box.

"Let's call him 'Babycake,'" she says and I laugh and click the belt in on my side.

Thirty-seven

When we get back, the barbecue is ready. There are plates of burgers and sausages and ribs and one labelled 'very vegan'. Pattie's music is still blaring out and she has made lots of fancy drinks. Jay passes them round. I take one. The glass has a lovely long stem but the drink is bright green with red bits floating in it.

"Don't worry if it's disgusting," says Jay. "Mum uses all this odd stuff. It has kale in it. Tip it in the bushes if you want!" I smile and take a sip. He watches me.

"It's different," I say, wincing a little and he laughs. Dana takes hers and pretends to gag.

Jay opens his presents. There are vouchers and a watch from his mum and a sports top from Clare and the cousins. He picks up my box, turns it round and round, looking for a tag.

"Oh," I say. "That's mine. Sorry." He says thanks and rips off the paper and opens the box.

"This is so cool." He holds up the football. It's an official Liverpool one. Tucker leans over and grunts his approval. I'm so proud of Dad. He got it spot on.

Paul strings up the piñata. It's a penguin piñata, black and white with a yellow beak, just like Jay's. It makes me smile. Pattie marks out a big 'safety hitting' area.

"Do you want to go first?" says Jay, handing a baseball bat to me.

"I'll be rubbish!" I say but I take it and whack it hard and it flies into the air, bits of crepe paper coming off it.

"Go on, Amy!" yells Paul. So I whack it again and a split starts to appear. I pass the bat over to Jay.

"My turn!" yells Dana and she grabs it from Jay and starts really beating it. The penguin flies into the air and spins round. The beak is squashed flat. A few sweets drop. Jay looks at me and smiles and raises his eyebrows as if this is always what Dana is like. I've never seen Dana like this – happy and having a good time. It's nice.

Tucker is next and with one whack, the poor penguin's tummy is ripped open and sweets start to scatter. Jay finishes the game with some hefty hits and we all dive to pick up the sweets.

Paul brings out the cake. It's a giant football pitch. One side of the grass is slightly dented.

"Think that's when Babycake slipped!" says Dana, leaning in to me.

"Yep!" I say and we both laugh a bit and I notice she has put her hair clip back in and I'm glad.

We all sing and Jay blows out the candles.

"We need a group photo!" says Pattie.

"I'll take it," I say.

"Absolutely not!" says Pattie. "We'll use that timer thing. Paul, can you set it up?" She puts her arm round me and moves me over to where everyone is starting to gather. She goes to help Paul balance his phone on the birdbath.

We all get into a huddle.

"Wait for the flashing red light!" shouts Paul. "Ten seconds after the first flash it will take!" He presses the button and runs into place. Tucker gets hold of Jay and lifts him high. Pattie and Clare clink glasses. Dana elbows me gently and points to the pile of piñata confetti and we scoop it up and let it fly over our heads. Paul yells *cheese*. The photo takes. He fetches the camera and shows us. It's a great shot. I wonder if it will make Jay's wall. Maybe it will be framed with a sign saying 'Birthday'.

Clare looks at her watch. "We need to get going," she says. "Tucker's got swim training." Dana makes a face. I think she just wants to stay here.

"I'll make a move too," says Pattie and she gathers her things. We all help to clear up a little and then leave together, each of us with slices of cake wrapped in foil.

"I'll see you soon," Dana says to me as she opens the car door. I nod and smile. "It was fun today," she says. "You know, getting the cake and stuff."

"Yeah," I say.

Dana waves from the back of the car. I wave back and Clare pulls away.

Jay kicks the new football in the air, over and over.

Pattie comes out with a box of bottles and juices to take home. She puts the box in the boot and then wraps herself around Jay. He lets go of the ball and it rolls away. I want to go home and leave them to say bye. But Pattie's car is blocking the drive and now they are standing in the only gap to get through. I look round for Captain, hoping to see him, to give me something to do. He's nowhere so I pick up the new ball that Jay has dropped, roll it round in my hands.

"Oh my!" Pattie suddenly shrieks. "Mr Penguin is out!"

"Yep!" Jay says. "Dad put him there this morning, for my birthday. We were telling the guys across the road about it and he got all, you know, gushy about it."

"Look, Amy!" says Pattie and she points to Jay's window. "Have you seen?" I walk forward and look up, putting one hand over my eyes to keep the sun out. The penguin has a party hat on and is holding a balloon, tied to one flipper. I smile. I'm not sure if I should say anything so I don't.

"Do you remember the beach scene, Jay?" says Pattie. "He had sunglasses, sun hat, a bucket. I think there were even pebbles on the windowsill. I loved that one!"

"Yep," says Jay. He picks up the ball and kicks it on to his knee.

"I've not embarrassed you, have I, love?" says Pattie and Jay turns and shakes his head.

"No, Mum, I was about seven," he says. "And it's only Amy."

It's only Amy. I feel so great he said that. I like being *only Amy*.

Pattie laughs and opens her car door. "See you both soon! So glad you could come today, Amy." I smile and say thanks. She sets off, beeps the horn.

Jay kicks the ball at me and I kick it back. It rolls down the drive towards the goalpost by the garage door and we both run after it.

Thirty-eight

"Roast Sunday lunch," says Pops, "followed by Jay coming over for a game. What a day!" He smiles at us both. He looks happy and I'm glad.

"That top," says Pops, pointing at Jay. "Did you wear it before? I think I've seen it before."

Jay looks down as if he needs to check which one he is wearing. He smiles at Pops and looks at the board, getting ready for his go. He picks up a coin. Stops. Tries. Stops.

"Take your time," says Pops. He sits down in his chair. I'm not sure if Pops means for Jay to take time in answering or to have his next go on the board. But it doesn't really matter.

"It's my favourite top," says Jay.

"Is it a special player?" says Pops, staring. "Springer?"

"Yeah," says Jay. "George Springer. Houston Astros team. Number four." He spins round to show Pops the number four on the back.

"Is that a football team?" I ask, picking out the next piece of jigsaw to try. We have started the sky again. With all the pieces of blue and orange and pink. I'm not very good at the whole shove ha'penny thing.

"Baseball," says Jay, lining up his coin. "He's my hero. Dad ordered me this shirt all the way from America."

"America," says Pops, heaving himself out of the chair and examining Jay's lanes on the board. "That's where Spinney went."

"Why did he go there?" I ask.

Pops lifts his eyes from the board and looks up, at the shelves and pictures and cuckoo clock. It's like he's lining up all the thoughts in his head, draining them, filtering them to find the right one. It's like that thing we did in science with the tray of sand, shaking it through the grid to see what dropped underneath.

"I think," says Pops calmly, as if the right thought has filtered through, "he needed a fresh start. It was tough for him back then. Had a few tricky times. I looked after him for a bit. So much easier now, as it should be."

"Oh," I say. I don't know what Pops means about things being easier now. I want to ask but then he carries on.

"Think it was Florida he ended up. I wonder if my Spinney ever met your ... what was it again?"

Jay hesitates.

"Springer," he says. "George Springer."

"We're a right pair aren't we, lad?" says Pops, reaching for the coins to take his turn. "You can't get the words out and I can't remember them."

Jay looks at him and for a second I'm worried he'll be upset but then he bursts out laughing and so does Pops. I smile and arrange the pile of blue and orange pieces and watch as Pops takes to the board, lining up the coins, deciding how to move it down the lane, exactly as he did it back in the smoky pub, all those years ago with his friend Spinney. I'm so glad Jay and Pops have had this time together. I'm so glad for them both.

♣ ♣ ♣

"Why's the Springer guy your hero?" I ask as Jay puts on his trainers to leave. He stands up and looks at me but I know he's just thinking, not about to speak. I know now. You get to know.

And then he says, "He has a stutter, just like me. And he helps kids who stutter."

I smile. "Joe Biden has one too," I say. "And Mum said he's the president."

Jay nods and opens the front door. "Not sure I'll ever be the president!" he says and he runs back over the road and goes straight to the lounge window, tapping at the glass to wake up Captain. Captain wakes and stretches and puts his nose to the window, arches his back against the glass. Jay turns round and waves at me. "Laziest cat ever!" he says and I laugh and close the door.

Thirty-nine

Mum's got perfume on and the jacket she wears when she needs to look smart. It's like we're going for an interview.

"I'm a bit nervous," I say.

"You're bound to be," says Mum.

"Oh, Amy," says Gran. "It will be amazing! How exciting to be the *only* person going round your super new school."

"It's the *worst* thing," I say, "to be the *only* person going round."

"Oh," says Gran. "Well, try and see it as being lucky you're able to *go* to school at all."

Sam grunts. "I can't wait to leave school and go and work in Kenya or Malawi."

I look at the clock, pull my top straight, dodge Maxi's outstretched hand, covered in porridge. "Dad knows what time to be there, doesn't he?"

"Yep," says Mum. "He phoned me just now asking where his blue shirt is. He's even got the iron out! He hasn't ironed a shirt for a whole year!" She gets a wipe and cleans Maxi's face and lifts him out of the high chair. He kicks his legs hard and arches his back.

"Are you sure Cassie and her mum will be able to cope with him?"

"Yep," says Mum. "Come on." We grab the bags and Mum checks Sam knows how to use Gran's ancient mobile phone.

"No need for that!" shouts Gran.

"It's just in case you sprain the *other* ankle," says Mum.

"Ridiculous," says Gran. "And we could easily have looked after Maxi too!"

"Maxi is never easy," says Mum. She kisses Gran and we walk to the car.

It takes an hour to get to Cassie's house. Mum lets me choose all the music and we sing and jig and tap the car and Maxi falls asleep. We pull up at Cassie's house and he is gently snoring. Mum gets the stroller out and transfers him, still asleep. We ring the bell and when Cassie answers we tell her to be super quiet and we push Maxi into the front hall. Cassie tucks his blanket around him, wedges his giraffe by his tummy. She leans in to me and whispers, "Hope you hate it."

I whisper back, "I'll try."

We close the door quietly and walk down the path.

"Cassie is so good with him," says Mum and I nod because she is.

We get in the car and pull away.

"I heard what she said," says Mum. "About hoping you hate it. That wasn't kind, I don't think."

I stare at the road ahead.

"She needs to grow up a little," says Mum. I glance at her and then look back at the road.

"I won't really try to hate it," I say. "Not much point now, is there?"

Mum reaches for my hand and squeezes it.

"I just said that for Cassie," I say.

"I know," says Mum. She starts to say something else but she stops and pulls her hand back to change gear. She puts on the radio and we drive through the village, past the turning for our old house. I catch a glimpse of the road sign and the tree with the yellow flowers. The flowers are dropping, the tree is losing its bright yellow spread, and it feels a long time now since we lived there.

Forty

Dad's car is in the visitor area at the school. We park beside him. He gets out when he sees us. Mum and Dad have a hug and a kiss and I make a vomit sound, spin round to check no one is watching.

"Look at you!" says Mum, smoothing Dad's collar. "Decent shirt and a pair of chinos. Haven't seen you that smart for quite a while!"

It's true. Dad has been in joggers or shorts since the accident.

"Big day," says Dad, pulling me in.

"It's not really," I say. "It's just to meet this stupid form tutor." I feel a bit bad saying that and I'm about to add that I'm excited to see the dance studio but Mum jumps in first.

"Amy!" she snaps, looking round to check no one has heard. She lowers her voice as if Thornberry has microphones planted in the car park trees. "You just said, just now in the car, that you were going to try and enjoy it. We are going with a positive attitude. This lovely man is coming in especially today to meet us and show us round, which he wouldn't have had to do if you had tried a bit harder to enjoy it back in October."

"Or if you hadn't told me I could go to Valley High."

We walk across the tarmac. An empty crisp packet blows past. The goalposts are all stacked up. We pass empty classrooms with chairs on desks and clean display boards.

We have to press a buzzer and wait to go in. I clutch my bag. My phone beeps.

"Sorry," I say quickly. I know they'll be annoyed about my phone. I grab it and put it on silent. It's Molly.

Hope it goes OK and u have fun!

A lady answers the door. She has a security thing around her neck, like Mum uses at work. We have to sign in on a big screen. There are lots of framed certificates and articles about the school on the wall.

"Impressive," says Dad, but he hasn't read any of them.

"Such a great school," says Mum, glancing around her. The articles could say: *Thornberry – worst school in history. One thousand pupils on strike. Children learn absolutely nothing at this terrible school* and they'd still think it all looked amazing.

"Mr Kaminski will be here in a minute," says the lady. She prints out visitor stickers for us to wear, which seems really silly as we are the only people here. I glance down the corridor. I recognize the break-out space from the big tour in the autumn. It looked enormous then. It looks even bigger now with no one in it.

"You must be Amy!"

We turn round to see a very, very tall man wearing jeans and a T-shirt. My parents look a bit overdressed. He shakes all of our hands.

"I've been so excited to meet you, Amy," he says.

OK, so I'm really not that special. I have a funny feeling that Mr Kaminski has been told about our rather odd situation. The one about me not wanting to come to this school.

I smile at him and say, "Thanks," which I think is what I'm meant to say. Mum rattles on about how grateful we are and how wonderful the school is. You'd think Thornberry was a holiday camp, the way she's talking.

"What do you teach, Mr Kaminski?" she asks. Poor guy. Here comes Mum's interrogation. She'll ask him what pets he has next or what his favourite thing is to eat.

"I teach music." He turns to me. "Do you like to sing or play anything, Amy?"

I shake my head.

"She played the violin for a term in Year Four," says Mum.

I glare at her. That's hardly going to excite Mr Kaminski.

"We're not really a musical family," says Mum. "Sorry. We're more books and games and nature and sciencey sort of things." And then for some reason the three of them get on to DT and building stuff and before I know it they're telling poor Mr Kaminski about our terrible house and the DIY and the three of them chat about plaster and swap tips about tiling and tile dividers.

I'm not sure Mr Kaminski is used to parents that talk as much as Mum.

"But!" says Mum, spinning round to face me as if she's *suddenly* realized the reason we are *actually* here. She raises her hand and points one finger in the air. "Amy *is* a fantastic dancer!" I glare at her. I can't believe she just said that.

"I'm not really," I say.

"Street dance, that's Amy's thing."

We haven't even left the hallway and Mr Kaminski knows Dad is tiling our grotty house and I do street dance and Mum hasn't a musical bone in her body.

"Fantastic," says Mr Kaminski. "I'll show you the dance studio on the tour." He hands me a pack of paper. "There are forms here for you to fill out at home. Some of it is online.

I'd do the uniform one pretty sharp. We've been a bit low on certain things. But more stock is coming in." I think of Rosie at the District Sports event and how she told me the pleated skirts had all run out and how I'd definitely left it too late.

We walk down the long corridors, poking our heads into empty rooms and science labs that smell. There's a computer room and a massive cafeteria and a gym the size of the field. Giant basketball hoops are at either end and I picture Jay racing down the squeaky floor, scoring a slam dunk.

"Is the dance studio near here?" I ask.

Mum beams at me as if my question means I have decided this is the school for me. So I walk in front of her, following Mr Kaminski.

"Just down here," he says. I'm glancing at the framed photos of the dance groups, all on one big board. Jazz, tap, street.

We go through double doors.

"Here we are!" says Mr Kaminski.

"Oh wow!" says Mum. She presses on the sprung floor and looks around her, gasping a little. You'd have thought we'd have arrived on the surface of a new planet.

"What do you think, Amy?" asks Mr Kaminski.

I nod and say, "Great."

It *is* great. I've never been in one like this. Jamila's dance studio is in the old village hall.

Mum and Dad walk across the room and test out the barre, running their hands along it as if they're admiring the secure fitting.

"I imagine you're probably a bit nervous," says Mr Kaminski, looking at me, his arms folded. "I know you don't know many people in Year Seven but I wanted to reassure you, Amy. There are two others in the form who don't know anyone at all. And we'll have lots of settling-in activities."

I nod and smile at him.

Mum calls out, "Look, Ames!" She points to a white poster. "Year Seven and Eight modern dance club. Monday lunchtimes!"

Mr Kaminski smiles and we set off again. I like him. He smiled at me as if to say, '*All new parents are like this, don't worry, it's not just yours.*' I stay next to him, my parents padding behind. Two other kids, brand new, don't know anyone at all. I wonder how. Have they just moved here? Are they like me and couldn't get into the school they wanted? There will be three of us. Three complete newbies. I wonder if we will be friends.

"Our form room!" says Mr Kaminski, opening a set of doors. "I think you'll be very happy here, Amy. We have a great view!" The room is upstairs with giant windows overlooking the field. The desks are all lined up, chairs pushed underneath. A bird lands on the outside sill, pecks at something. It makes me think of Sam.

On the way back to the hall, we pass the theatre and the stage area and then we are back in the front hall and Mr Kaminski says goodbye and that he will see me in a few weeks. We peel off our visitor stickers and go back to the cars.

"Well, that was fantastic!" says Dad.

"Amazing," says Mum. "What a nice man."

"Let's go for a quick coffee," says Dad.

We drive away in Dad's car. The back seat is covered in paint pots and bags of plaster and a long pole with a sponge on one end. I move it so it's upright. It reminds me of Paul's golf club and it makes me smile.

I stare out of the car window. Mr Kaminski *was* really great. The dance studio *was* exciting. There will be *other* Year 7 kids who know no one. Jay will be there.

"Bet you can't wait to join that dance club, Amy," says Mum, glancing back at me.

I don't reply. Saying anything good out loud just seems too hard right now and I don't know why.

When we reach the big main road Dad reaches out and holds Mum's hand. I can see him squeeze it as if to say, '*It will all be fine*.' I don't want Mum and Dad to have any more worries. These past few years have all been about too many worries.

We go to our favourite café and order breakfast baps. Dad tells me about the house and shows me photos of freshly plastered walls and a new toilet and the gap where the kitchen wall came down. I can see Dad's builder friend Ghaf and Darcey the electrician, laying out wires. She has a long ginger plait and dungarees.

"You had so much help," I say. Dad smiles and nods his head a little and says, "I can't tell you Ames. It's been like that show on TV, the number of guys that showed up."

"Bet Darcey kept them all in check," says Mum.

"*No one* messes with Darcey," says Dad and we all laugh. I rest my head on his shoulder and it's good to feel his shirt against my skin.

Forty-one

Maxi is crawling round Cassie's garden, his little bottom up in the air. Cassie is with him, picking him up and setting him off again like a wind-up toy.

"We changed his nappy," says Nicky. "And he ate all the lunch you gave me."

"Can't thank you enough," says Mum. Maxi stops and sits back and stares at Mum. He's heard her voice. He heads straight for her and then starts pulling at her legs, whining.

"So typical!" says Mum. "Sees me and becomes all needy!"

"Coffee?" says Nicky.

"Sorry," says Mum, picking up Maxi. "Love to, but I have to get back for a work call."

Cassie collects up Maxi's toys and giraffe and joins us.

"How was Thornberry?" asks Nicky, looking at me.

"Good," I say.

Cassie passes Maxi his giraffe and he grabs it and sucks on its ear.

"I've heard it's a great school," says Nicky.

"She doesn't know anyone," says Cassie, picking at her nails.

We all head towards the house.

"Actually, Cassie," says Mum, turning to face her, "she does now. Amy knows Dana, her friend from dance, and Jay. They're cousins. She even went to Jay's party on Saturday."

Ouch. Here we go. Thanks, Mum. Cassie darts me a quick look.

"Oh," says Nicky. "That's fantastic, Amy! A few friendly faces is all you need."

I keep walking into the house.

I can feel Cassie next to me, all prickly. She'll hate the fact she didn't know about the party. I went to a sleepover at Sophia's once, just me and her, and Cassie didn't talk to me for two days. I open Maxi's bag of toys, rearrange them a little.

"Let me just get his bottle and lunch things," says Nicky and Mum follows her into the kitchen.

Cassie and I walk towards the hall. She says nothing to me. Nothing at all. She yanks Maxi's stroller from under the stairs and opens the front door.

"Thanks, Cass," says Mum, joining us. "You're a superstar!"

Cassie forces out a smile. She folds Maxi's blanket and straightens the stroller straps and pulls back the sunshade.

I feel guilty about the party and I know I shouldn't.

"See you soon," I say and she nods.

Mum walks past with Maxi. Cassie squeezes his hand.

"I'll put him in the car," Mum says. "We need to get going."

I nod and collapse the stroller. Cassie and I walk down the path together.

"Was it a good party?" she says very quietly, so I hardly hear. She stares out across the street. She can't look at me.

"It wasn't really a party. It was just a small thing with a cake and a piñata."

"What, that thing you bash?"

"Yeah," I say.

"They always have horrid sweets inside," she says.

"They were OK actually," I say.

"Nice," she says, with a little smile. She tucks her hair behind her ears, rocks on her feet a little. Mum takes the stroller and puts it in the car, glancing at her watch and dashing in to start the engine.

"It was fun," I say. "Jay is great. And Dana is nice too."

I stare at her. I want her to be a good friend. I want her to say she's pleased for me.

She doesn't say anything.

"It's good to make new friends, Cass. You're doing it too. Sahira and Zoe."

Cassie looks down the street. She shrugs a little as if she's not sure she agrees.

Mum beeps the horn. I climb in and we pull away.

I wave at Cassie. She raises one hand and turns away.

I feel sorry for her and I know I shouldn't.

♣ ♣ ♣

"How was it?" asks Jay. He polishes his coin and looks at Pops and makes a face like he's in the Wild West, about to draw his pistol.

"Fine," I say. I'm doing the jigsaw. I played one round of shove ha'penny but I only got two chalk marks.

"Did you see the gym?" he says, sliding his coin down the board. "Whoa! Spot on!" He fist-pumps the air.

"Yeah," I say. "But I didn't find it *that* exciting."

"I don't mean the gym!" yells Jay. "I got a *perfect* float!" he says, spinning round, smiling.

"*Again…*" says Pops, raising his eyes to the ceiling.

"Who's your form tutor?" says Jay.

"This really tall guy. Mr Kaminski."

Jay stops and stares at me.

"You're *so* lucky. He's really cool. He runs the basketball team," says Jay. "My mate Ben is in his form."

"Who do you have?" I ask.

He groans and says, "Mrs Rumpthistle. She teaches chemistry."

I feel a bit sorry for Mrs Rumpthistle.

"Why don't you like her?"

He lines up his next coin. "She's OK. But she doesn't play basketball."

"How do you know?" says Pops.

Jay smiles and turns round and says, "Well, she's very small and about sixty years old!"

"She might whizz in between everyone," I say. "Like you can do in netball sometimes. Cassie's brilliant at it."

"I'll let you know," says Jay. He shoves his coin and it nudges his other into place, which gives him two perfect beds. "Bingo!" he yells.

Pops helps Jay add up his score on the board. "Crazy you should be so good, Spinney," says Pops. "When you've hardly played!" He collects up the coins and mutters to himself, "*Spinney, Spinney, flick the coin in its bed, float it, Spinney, or build it instead.*"

Forty-two

Mum wakes me up with a glass of juice.

"Hope you're OK on that bed on the floor!" she says.

"Yep," I murmur. "I've kind of got used to it."

"Oh, Ames, I'm sorry. Not long now. Home soon."

I turn over and snuggle down.

"Right," says Mum, sitting on the floor next to me. "Listen up. I've just had a phone call and I need to run something by you."

My eyes flick open. What's she done now? Told the neighbours I'll do a street dance show? Signed me up for a three-night Thornberry settling-in camp?

I grunt to tell her I'm listening.

"Helen just phoned."

"Who?" I turn slightly so I can hear better.

"Helen, Molly's mum."

"Oh."

"She and Ravi are coming over this way to pick up a new

car. She realized it was close to us here and they thought if they brought Molly and Cassie with them, you three girls could meet up. Maybe go for a milkshake at that great place you told me about where you got Jay's cake?"

I pull the duvet back and sit up a bit.

"And you've agreed it?" I ask. I like the idea. I want to see Molly. But I'm fed up with Mum just sorting stuff without checking.

"No," she says, snapping a bit. "I haven't. Because I seem to have got in a bit of trouble this week 'agreeing' stuff so I said I'd talk to you and I'd just check that we didn't have plans today as we had thought about going to the zoo."

"The zoo!"

Mum stares at me. "It was a little white lie so I could check with you first if the plan works."

I sit up and take the glass of juice and take a sip. I lean in to Mum. She strokes my hair.

"Sounds great," I say.

Mum kisses me and stands up and salutes and says in a sort of posh secretary voice, "Very good, ma'am. I shall return the call and make suitable arrangements," and then she tucks the duvet back around me and tells me to come down when I'm ready.

Forty-three

Molly and her parents arrive at two. There are drops of summer rain in the air.

"Jump in," says Ravi. "She's only got a few miles left in her!" The car splutters and churns out black smoke. I wave at Mum and make a face out of the window as if I'm about to ride the dodgems. She laughs but she's watching the car as if she's worried we won't make it to the cake shop.

"How's Jay?" says Cassie, staring at his house.

"Great," I say.

Molly is in the middle. She glances at me and rolls her eyes.

Cassie shows us her new bag. It has this charging thing in it for her phone. We don't say much. I think she thought we'd say more.

Helen twists round from the front seat. "Your mum said you went on a tour of Thornberry yesterday, Amy."

"Yep," I say.

"How was it?" she asks.

"Fine," I say.

Cassie sniffs a bit and hugs her bag. "Do you think you'll have to go there?" she says. "To Thornberry?"

I stare out of the window and nod gently. No one speaks for a bit. The windscreen wipers scrape on the glass, leaving smeary lines. The car stalls at the lights. Ravi starts it up again.

"Tell you something," says Ravi, revving the engine so hard it sounds like we might take off. "I went to a different school than my local friends. And there was an upside, you know." He turns the corner. We are all listening very close, as if Ravi has the golden answer to all this. "It kind of made those friendships stronger. Because you weren't involved with all the school stuff. You know – who's in, who's out. You were just mates because you liked being with each other." Molly rests her head on my shoulder. "Me and Baz are *still* best mates and I only went to school with him when I was six."

"You two," says Helen, "are not an example to uphold! You're like a pair of toddlers."

"We are not!" yells Ravi.

"Last time Baz was round, you and he had a squirty cream fight!" We all smile.

"You've got to have a squirty cream fight," says Ravi. "Not a good night otherwise."

"Not normally at the age of forty-two, Rav," says Helen, but she's laughing and so are we. Molly shakes her head as if she can't believe her dad can be so silly.

Ravi pulls into the car park.

"Is this the right place?" asks Helen.

"Yeah," I say, "the café is right there." I point to where we got Jay's cake. It's raining quite a bit now. The café windows are steamed up a little.

"Perfect," says Helen. "The car garage is literally on the other side of the street. We won't be long." There's lots of chat about phones being charged and not leaving the shop and what to do if the whole shopping parade burns down and we have to run.

"Say goodbye to the old girl," says Ravi.

Molly strokes the seats and checks there is nothing in the seat compartment. "We went to the theme park in this car, didn't we?" she says. "The five of us, for my birthday."

"Don't remind me," says Cassie and we all giggle. "Still have nightmares about that trip."

"I have never seen so much sick," says Helen. "You had to be wrapped in that blanket, Cassie, to get home, remember? You'd been so ill, bless you."

"It was that roller coaster," says Cassie. "Upside down so many times I'm sure my stomach turned inside out."

"Well, everything in your stomach *came* out, that's for sure!" says Ravi and we all laugh.

We get out and dash in to dodge the rain.

"Wow, this is cool," says Molly.

We wait in the queue and when we get to the till we order cakes and milkshakes. It takes a while to pay because Cassie's purse gets tangled in her new charging thing and she drops everything. She's so pink and flustered by the time we've paid that she has little underarm sweat patches.

"You OK?" I say. She nods and we find a table.

"Can you really charge your phone in your bag?" I ask, to try and make her feel better.

"Yeah," she says, putting her purse away. "I told you that." She's a bit sulky now.

"Tell me about the dance studio," says Molly and I tell them about the springy floor and the empty classrooms and Mr Kaminski and the uniform shortage. Molly smiles at me the whole time, taking in every word. Cassie sits with her arms folded, staring at the table, her eyes flicking around the room. It's like she doesn't want to hear anything about it.

"It sounds great," says Molly.

I shrug.

"We can still see each other," says Cassie, nudging the table slightly. She leans forward and tips out the little pot of sugar sachets and layers them up, like that game with the wooden blocks. "Like Ravi said, we're still triple besties."

We sit very quietly for a bit. No one knows what to say. It's like we all know it won't be quite the same.

A giant tray arrives with our order. Cassie perks up. She has the biggest cake and all the trimmings on her milkshake. We talk about Molly's party and what we will wear and whether we should watch a movie or not. Molly tells us who she's invited. She says Jess's name and Cassie just nods and stirs her drink, picking off the toppings with her straw.

The little bell on the café door rings and I look over and my breath catches a bit because Dana walks in with a girl I've never seen before. She has a purple streak in her hair. They get in the queue.

"What do you think?" says Molly.

"Sorry?" I say, slurping on my straw even though there's nothing left.

"About having a nail bar. At the party. Mum said we could buy five or six colours and some stick-on gems."

"Sounds cool," I say and I slant my eyes to watch the two girls. They're getting near to the ordering bit. "Shall we go?"

Molly checks her phone. "Mum hasn't texted yet."

·"I haven't finished," says Cassie. She's cut her cake into little pieces and is only halfway through.

"Do you think we should do pedicures too?" says Molly. "Mum has one of those foot baths."

Cassie shudders. "I *hate* feet. They make me feel so yuck, just looking at them." She shoves in several pieces of cake. I look over at the till. Dana is ordering. Purple Streak is on her phone. The lady behind the counter is writing down what they want.

Cassie picks up a piece of chocolate cake on her fork. "The chunks are so good!" she says. I glance back at the till. They are paying. They'll need a table soon. The café is super busy.

It's like the two sides of my life are here, in this café, with just a few squares of checked flooring between us. I don't like it. It makes me feel super hot.

Molly's phone beeps. "OK," she says. "Let's finish up. They're ready." Cassie wipes her straw round her glass and licks it. She scoops up the last of the crumbs.

"Come on, Cass," I say.

"All right," she says. "What's the big rush?"

I get up quick but my jacket gets caught on the chair. We turn to go and Dana is right there. With Purple Streak.

"Oh. Hi," I say.

"Hi," says Dana. Her hair is up in this twisty thing. There are two strands hanging down either side of her face. But just two strands. Not the normal curtains.

"Are you having cake?" I ask. Silly question.

"Yeah," says Dana. She's gone a little red. She turns to Purple Streak.

"This is Amy. She's an incredible dancer and she's coming to Thornberry." She glances at me and smiles a little. I smile back and give Purple Streak a little wave, which then feels a bit silly so I put my hand in my pocket.

"Hi!" says Purple Streak. "That's cool."

"Well, she doesn't want to," says Cassie, leaning in and talking quite loud. "She wants to come to Valley High with us, don't you, Ames?"

I look at Cassie. Why did she have to say that?

"Um, I was hoping to," I say. "But I don't think I can."

"Do you have your skirt?" asks Purple Streak. "Someone told me they ran out last week."

"Not yet," I say. "Do you have yours?" Of course she does, Amy. Everyone else got sorted ages ago. Like Rosie.

"No, I still haven't got anything!" she says and she laughs. "Not like Dana. She's had her stuff for months!"

"I'm glad I'm not the only one," I say.

"What form are you in?"

"Um, Mr Kaminski."

"Wow, same!" says Purple Streak. "I'm Summer, by the way."

Molly's phone beeps.

"Mum's outside," she says. "We have to go."

We all say bye and when I get to the café door, I look back and wave at Summer and Dana and they wave back. And then I check in the mirror and they don't make any silly faces or copy me. They just take off their jackets and sit down.

Forty-four

We stand and wait for the car, the rain gently falling.

"Never met *anyone* called Summer," says Cassie. "And does everyone at Thornberry have weird hair?"

"What do you mean?" I ask.

Cassie shrugs and looks away and stares at the menu in the window.

I so want to tell Cassie to get lost.

"I thought they seemed nice," says Molly. "There's a girl called Autumn at my scouts." She links her arm in mine and I squeeze her tight.

The car pulls up. It's bright red. We climb in. It smells shiny, brand-new, like a pencil case in September.

We are quiet all the way back. The sun comes out, gleaming off the wet roads.

I think about Summer and Dana and then I lean my head on Molly's shoulder and she leans her head against mine.

When we get back to Gran and Pops' house, Jay is out front, shooting hoops.

"Are we coming in?" says Cassie.

Ravi looks at his watch. "Sorry, Cass, we've got to get back."

"Thanks for the trip," I say as I climb out.

Molly waves at me. "See you on Saturday!" she shouts and they pull off.

Jay comes over the road, bouncing the ball, checking for cars.

"Want to shoot some hoops?" he says. I nod and put my bag by the door and we spend a bit of time out front. Captain is on the grass, watching us.

"He's free!" I say.

"Yep," says Jay, jumping as he shoots. "Couldn't keep him in any longer."

I smile and he passes the ball to me.

"How come Cassie was here?" says Jay.

"Oh, Molly's parents were buying a new car at a garage over here. We went for a drink while they picked it up."

He passes me the ball and I shoot and the ball actually goes *in* the hoop. It bounces back towards Jay. He catches it and turns to say something but for the first time in a while nothing comes. He bounces the ball and turns to shoot instead. I want to know what he was going to say. I wait. But we just carry on playing.

"I saw Dana," I say. I fetch the ball from by the garage door.

"Did you?" says Jay. "She and Clare are *always* shopping."

I shoot. It misses and bounces off the ring.

"She was with a friend," I say. Jay would normally chase my miss but he leaves it, lets it roll away on to the grass, spins to look at me.

"Which friend?" he asks.

"Um, her name was Summer."

He moves away to get the ball, seems to relax again and says, "With the purple bit in her hair?"

"Yeah."

"That's OK." It's an odd thing to say. As if Dana being out with a friend isn't normally OK.

"She seemed nice."

"She is. Summer's great."

I like the way Jay says that. Summer did seem really lovely.

Captain walks past and Jay picks him up and tickles him under the chin. "There are a few girls that have been a bit mean to Dana. She kept trying to be part of their group and it just got worse."

Jay bounces the ball to me, Captain still hooked under his arm. I turn to the hoop and toss it high.

I think about the group of girls in the café when we got the cake. I didn't like them. They made Dana very nervous.

The ball bounces towards the garage door. I chase it and pick it up and I'm about to throw it to Jay but he's cuddling Captain, rubbing him under the chin. It makes me think of Sophia and her dog Jasper. He loves to be tickled under the chin. They got Jasper from the rescue centre. He was very shy at first. It took him months to sit still and be stroked.

Maybe Dana is a bit like Jasper. She needs time to trust again. Maybe Dana thought people might never be nice to her again.

Forty-five

"Look what Gran found, Amy!" says Pops. I switch on a lamp. The front room is just getting dark now as the sun goes down. It bathes the room in golden orange, the sun dropping behind Jay's roof.

He brushes the dust off the lid of the old shoebox and opens it. We spend a few minutes looking at the newspaper clippings and black-and-white photos, Pops passing each one to me with a smile or a nod. And then he holds up a photo of two men.

"Me and Spinney." He turns the photo over. "No date. Shame. Must have been in the sixties. Just before we finished our apprenticeship."

I stare at the photo of Spinney and I can completely see why Pops thinks Jay is so like him. He has the same ears and dimple in the chin and shape of the cheeks.

"You should show this to Jay!" I say.

"Who?" says Pops. He puts the photo back in the box

and closes the lid.

"You know, Pops. My friend Jay who's been coming to play shove ha'penny with us. Jay from across the road. You call him Spinney Jay sometimes, because he looks just like Spinney."

Pops stares at the board and then he looks back at me and he says, "I don't remember."

I pick up the five coins on the board, ready to be played with. "He's been learning the rules, Pops. You taught him."

Pops nods and sits back in his chair and mutters to himself, "*Spinney, Spinney, come quick, don't be late. Spinney, race fast, before they close the gate.*"

And then he turns and looks at his books on the shelf. The safari guide is propped up, ready to be put away, next to the Masai Mara guide. "We saw the baboons, didn't we?"

"Yeah, at the safari park last week."

He stares at me. And just at that moment the sun dips behind Jay's house, the golden glow gone, the warmth taken from the room.

"And cheetahs, didn't we?" says Pops. "We searched every day and we saw the cheetah on the last day."

"Yes, Pops," I say and I leave the room and fetch Gran because I know Pops needs to talk to Gran now, to pin him down to that day, that time and make the spinning stop.

Forty-six

"You can buy boards, you know," says Jay. "I looked online. I might buy one with my birthday money."

Pops flicks his coin down the lane and it sits perfectly in the bed. He stands up and smiles and says, "What do you think, Spinney?"

"I-I…" says Jay. We wait. "I think you're a master!"

"No, Spinney's the shuff master," he says. He takes the photo of the two of them from the mantelpiece and shows it to Jay. "Here you go."

"Gran found the photo yesterday," I say.

Jay leans in and smiles. "I suppose he does look a bit like me."

"Yes," says Pops. "Yes." And he props the photo back up and Jay gets ready for his go.

"Last one," he says, lining up the coin.

"Do you go to your mum's tonight?" I ask.

"Yeah," says Jay. "She's coming soon. We're going camping on Friday."

"Wow!" I say and it's odd because I can't imagine Pattie camping.

"It's glamping really," says Jay, lining up his next coin. "Big, heated tepee tents with proper beds."

"Sounds fun."

I finish off the big section of blue and pink and orange sky. The jigsaw is nearly complete again. Just the cottage roof to go. And then there's a knock on the front door. Pops and Jay are adding up the scores, laughing about the final go.

"Thanks for all the games, Pops," says Jay. "I'd love to play again when I'm staying with Dad, later in the summer."

Pops looks at Jay for a moment. And then he nods and collects the coins and pats Jay, very gently, on the back.

"Good lad," he says. "Good lad, Spinney."

I wonder how much Pops will remember, later in the summer.

"I'll probably forget the rules," says Jay.

"I'll write them down for you," says Pops. "Our version. Spinney and me."

It's funny that Pops is going to write them down so that *Jay* will remember them. I wonder if Pops will forget the rules one day. And need a copy for himself. I hope not.

"That would be amazing," says Jay. "Then I'd always have it with my board, when I buy one."

Pops nods and says, "Good idea." But then he looks at me and then at Jay and I can tell he's lost again, lost the thread.

Mum shouts from the hall.

"Jay, it's your mum!"

"Bye then," says Jay. Pops lifts one hand.

Pattie has a bunch of flowers and a bottle of wine.

"From me and Paul," she says. "Jay has had such fun. He doesn't have any granddads so meeting Pops is such a bonus. He's loved the vintage game."

"It's not vintage," says Jay. "I told you. You can buy boards today."

And then Pattie holds out a present for me.

"Hope this is OK, Amy! Dana said you loved dance and I thought this looked good but please just say if I've got it wrong."

I unwrap the parcel. It's tied with red ribbon. It's a dance top. It's the black and silver top I'd seen all those weeks ago, the one I'd really wanted.

"Gosh," says Mum. "That's so kind of you. Really no need." She leans in and pulls the sleeve straight and I can tell she recognizes it.

"Amy's been so great," says Pattie. "You all have. Helping Paul and giving Jay something else to do while he's here!"

"Thanks so much," I say.

They turn to go. Pattie's perfume drifts across the doorway.

"I'm so glad," she says, looking back, "that you and Jay are going to Thornberry together."

"Yeah," I say.

"And she's so lucky," says Jay. "Her form tutor is Mr Kaminski!"

Pattie smiles.

"See you," says Jay and he waves at me and I smile and wave back.

Mum closes the door.

"What a lovely lady," she says. She takes her hair band off her wrist and puts her hair up. "It was so kind of her to buy you that top."

I lean in to Mum and hug her tight.

"I actually prefer the purple one you got me," I say.

She hugs me back and then tickles me, right down my side where it makes me squirm. "Fibber," she says.

"I'm not fibbing!" I shriek. She's tickling both sides now, both of us in hysterics, me gasping for breath.

"You fib through your teeth!" she says, both of us laughing so hard that Sam appears from the garden wondering what all the fuss is about and Maxi follows, crawling super fast down the hallway towards Mum. And then we have to stop because Pops stumbles out of the lounge upset, asking for Gran and panicking that we have hurt ourselves.

Forty-seven

I wake up late. The house is quiet and I hear the cuckoo clock. Faint but clear. Ten cuckoos. One after the other. No early banging car doors today or Paul yelling at Jay to get his boots or his lunch.

Mum knocks on my door. "Ames, can you just mind Maxi for two minutes while I have a shower?" She opens the door and passes him to me. "Gran's physio is coming soon. Thought we'd go to the park."

Maxi is clean and wiped down and smells of baby stuff. He's clutching his giraffe. I snuggle into him and open the book Mum has passed to me. He drops his giraffe and puts his fingers though the holes on the page to make the legs of a lion and roars, his head tipped back. We look at the monkeys and the zebra and then Maxi gets restless and crawls over to the windowsill. I peel myself up and follow him, pull back the curtain, look out to Jay's house. The basketball is by the garage door. Captain is sitting on the fence. Jay's curtains are half closed.

And then I gasp a little and my breath catches and I lean out further, as if that extra little bit of space I'm filling will give me a better view.

The penguin is back. He's propped up with one flipper resting on the Liverpool ball and the other on a giant packet of Thai sweet chilli crisps. He is wearing the Astros top, the sleeves rolled up over each flipper. I smile and laugh. I wonder if Jay has left the penguin out for Paul, like when he was little. But I don't think so. I really don't.

I think he's left him there for me.

Mum knocks again.

"You OK? Just going to get dressed."

"We're great," I say and I pick up Maxi, scoop up his giraffe from the bed. "Look," I say. "Look." But he just pulls on the net and screeches a little and sucks on his giraffe's ear. I hold him tight to me, swaying a little, smiling at the penguin with the football and the crisps.

Forty-eight

"She's very pleased with my progress," says Gran, waving goodbye to the physiotherapist and closing the front door firmly. "Bossy thing, that young girl."

"Needs to be with you," says Mum, parking the stroller in the front hall. Maxi is fast asleep, his giraffe under his chin. "The park was heaving. He played for ages on that slide he loves."

Sam holds up his plastic pot to show Gran. "That river has so much wildlife. Look at all the creatures!" He takes it through to the back garden. "Don't worry – we're going back tomorrow to put them back in."

They both watch him go, smiling in that way they do with Sam. As if he's going to be the next David Attenborough and save a thousand dying species.

"So," says Mum, tucking the blanket round Maxi. "You really think you'll cope OK after Saturday?"

"Yes," says Gran. "I'm off the crutches. You're a phone

call away. It's not the ankle I'm worried about." She strokes Maxi's hair. "It's the company I'll miss."

"You have Pops," I say.

"Yes. I do," she says resting her head on Mum's shoulder. "But I miss his company too."

She takes a tissue from her pocket. We're quiet for a moment, the three of us huddled close, watching Maxi, so deeply asleep.

"I know," says Mum, gently wrapping one arm around Gran. "I know. We'll have to see how things go over the next few months." She puts the brake on the stroller. "You've always been super independent but things are different now. I think you should move closer to us. I might start looking into it."

Gran shrugs. "Maybe," she says and she wanders away to the kitchen.

"I think that would be good, Mum," I say.

Mum nods. "I know. And that's the first time she's given the idea a 'maybe'. It's always been a flat 'no' before. Progress."

I go to find Pops in the front room.

"This cottage roof," he says. "So many tiles the same shape and size and colour."

I smile and help find the next few pieces. We are nearly finished. The door is still in the box, complete from last time.

"Do you think the sky or the cottage is harder, Pops?" I ask.

"The sky," says Pops, sliding in the chimney piece. "Always the sky."

Mum pops her head round the door.

"I'm just finishing the school forms. Can you come here for a sec, Ames?"

"I'll be right back, Pops."

Mum is sitting at the kitchen table, surrounded by paper. "I need to put an emergency contact down that isn't me or Dad. We can't really put Gran any more and Uncle Jack lives too far away. How about Molly's mum, Helen?"

I nod.

"Yep. That's fine."

We fill in other stuff. The forms have Thornberry written all over them.

"I met a nice girl the other day. She was with Dana."

I'm expecting Mum to do her normal giddy, overexcited thing. But she just smiles and taps her pen against the table and says, "I'm glad. Is she going into Year Seven too?"

"She's in my form. She's called Summer."

"Cool name."

"I thought that," I say. "I'd like a cooler name. Amy is so normal."

Maxi cries out from his stroller.

"We could rename you," says Mum. "How about Tornado or Hurricane?" She kisses my head. "Or Precious." And she leaves to sort out Maxi and I think Precious sounds a really lovely name.

When I go back to Pops, he has finished the roof and the sky. The door slips in easily, each of the little corners slotting into place.

"We did it, Pops!" I say.

Pops stares at it, scanning the sky and the cottage and the pathway. I'm worried he will swipe it away again, but he doesn't. "We can do it again," he says.

"We have to leave on Saturday," I say.

"Oh, I don't know about that."

"We'll be back soon though. We can do it again then."

"Yes, that'd be good."

Gran calls to say lunch is ready.

"Dragon," says Pops and he turns to me and smiles.

Forty-nine

"They're all out, Sam," I say. "I'm sure of it." We've been here for ages. I'm starting to get really bored.

"I just need to swill it out once more," says Sam. He's kneeling next to the river, swiping a long stick across the surface, seeing what he can catch.

"Come on," I say. "Let's go."

"Why?" he says.

"Maxi will be restless soon." I look back. Mum is leaning against a tree. Maxi is in his stroller clutching a big, soggy biscuit.

"Five more minutes," he says. "Did you know, Ames, bacteria is vitally important to the river ecosystem?"

"No, I didn't," I say.

"Not that horrid sort of bacteria," he says, nodding to a pile of rubbish on the other side of the bank. "The good sort."

I don't say anything. I don't know anything about rivers.

"I love rivers," he says.

"I know."

"Ames."

I turn back. "Yep?"

He is digging in the mud on the bank.

"Can I ask you something?"

"Yeah."

I think he's going to ask me about the river or the creatures or good bacteria.

"Are you OK about going to Thornberry?" He pushes the stick into the riverbed, scraping it along the bottom. "I know you really wanted to go to Valley High. Was Thornberry that bad?" He turns round and looks at me, as if he wants to see what face I make. And I realize that maybe Sam is thinking about it all a bit more now. That he won't be able to go to school with his friends. That this will be him in a few years' time.

I sigh a little. "You know what, Sammy? It was actually really great."

He smiles and turns back to the water. "That's good," he says.

"They have loads of outdoor space and I saw a poster for an eco club and rewilding group."

"Really?" he says, spinning round.

"Yep," I say and I feel bad because I hadn't really checked out the poster. I wish I had. For Sam.

Mum calls us to make a move. We join her and head for home and I walk with Sam and I ask about the creatures that he found in the river.

"You don't have to ask, Ames," he says.

I nudge him with my shoulder and say, "I know I don't have to. I'm interested."

And this time, I really am.

Fifty

Pops stands in the doorway, staring at the car which is packed up and ready to go. The sun is bright and hot, everything coated in warmth.

"He doesn't understand," says Gran. "I'm not sure he knows what's happening today."

"Mmm," says Mum, shifting Maxi on to the other hip. "It's confusing for him. We've been here a while." She wraps her arm around Gran. "I'm going to have a little look at houses near us."

Gran says nothing. She just leans in to Mum and shrugs a little and nods.

There is a shriek from the back of the house, a door slams and Sam thunders through the hall.

"I got it! I got it!" He presses buttons, thrusts the trap cam under Mum's nose. "The hazel dormouse. Look! Right there!" Mum leans forward, shields her eyes to see the screen better. Gran and I lean in to watch. I catch a tail flash by.

"Amazing!" says Gran.

"Fantastic!" says Mum. "How do you know it's definitely a dormouse?"

Sam sits down under the shady porch, watches the film again and again.

"I just do," he says. He taps his knees. "I can't believe it. Look, along that branch. We need to phone the endangered species people. Right now and tell them!"

"When we're home, Sam. We'll do it straight away, OK?"

He nods.

"I have the number," he says and he watches the film again, fists clenched.

"I'm pleased for you, Sammy," I say, rustling his hair.

Mum walks to the car, straps Maxi into his seat and tucks the giraffe in his hands.

"We'll be over very soon," says Mum to Gran. "And just shout if that ankle plays up again!"

Sam peels himself up and we hug Gran and Pops. Pops turns and walks back into the house. We climb in the car. Mum gets in too, sorts out the radio, finds her favourite channel. And then we all turn round and wave and Pops is back on the front step, holding the jigsaw box high so I can see it. His shirt has popped out of his trousers, his vest all scrunched underneath. Mum starts to pull away. I wind down my window.

"We'll do it next time, Pops!" I shout and he smiles and waves. The box is hard to hold with one hand. The lid slips and the pieces start falling out from the open corner, a little stream of them, falling on to Pops' feet, scattering across the pathway, a couple bouncing off Spikey the hedgehog.

Fifty-one

The skip is still on the drive, piled high with rubbish. I can just see past it to the front of the house. Dad has tied balloons on the door. It's the same front door. Cracked and peeling. But it's about the only thing that looks the same. All the old plaster on the front of the house has been stripped. The brickwork is red and warm and there is a man on a ladder doing things to the edges of the bricks.

Mum parks on the road and beeps the horn. Dad comes round the side of the house. He's in shorts and a T-shirt.

"You're home!" he yells, slipping past the skip. "Let the chaos ensue!" Sam jumps out and throws himself at Dad. Mum climbs out and they hug and she peels Maxi out of his seat. I stay in the car, press my head against the window, and stare at the skip.

I think of the house where Jasmine lives now, with the white banisters and my clouds on the ceiling.

"My bug hotel has gone," says Sam.

"It's been moved," says Dad. "To the end of the garden. To your wildlife patch."

"You didn't?" says Mum, smiling at him.

"How could I not?" says Dad, taking Maxi and burying his face in his neck. Sam runs round the side, to the garden.

"Come on, Ames," says Mum, tapping on the window.

I open the door.

"Come and see," says Dad, passing Maxi back to Mum. "We've made a decent start."

There is banging from inside the house and a loud shout from an upstairs window.

I follow them inside.

They have knocked down a wall, stripped the horrid shiny wallpaper, ripped up the old carpets.

"What's that smell?" I ask.

"Plaster," says Dad. "A lot of fresh, new plaster on almost every wall."

The kitchen has been taken out. Every bit of it. New double doors go on to the garden.

"What do you think, Ames?" says Dad, wrapping his arm around me, shifting a bit of mess to one side with his foot as if to tidy a bit, make it neater. "The new kitchen goes in next week. I've had so much help. From everyone." He smiles at me, which pulls his little scar on his lip.

I nod and lean in to him and say, "Amazing," and then Mum asks him about the wiring for the kitchen units and they start talking about plug sockets and she gets a little tearful staring out at the garden.

I leave them and go upstairs. I peep in the bathroom. It's all been stripped out and a new toilet and bath are in place, a pile of tiles stacked by the side. It reminds me of Mr Kaminski and the chat about tile dividers, whatever they are. Dad's friend Filip is in Sam's room, smoothing plaster on to the wall with a funny-looking trowel. He sees me and says hi and I wave a little.

My bedroom door is shut. The wooden letters spelling out 'Amy' are there, slightly tilted. I straighten them and smile, remembering Jay's tilted penguin. I open the door. And then I gasp, very loudly, my breath trapped. I drop my bag.

New, soft carpet, cream walls, a bed with white struts on the headboard, a blanket of stars and stripes, fairy lights strung across the wall. I take it in, look around me, smell the newness, the freshness. I walk over to the bed and push down on it, pick up one of the cushions. And then I sit on the edge, stare at the walls, the windows, my books stacked on the new shelving unit.

I lie back and close my eyes.

Open them again.

On the ceiling are the fluffiest, dreamiest white clouds.

There is a gentle knock on the door.

Dad comes in. "You like it?"

"It's perfect," I say and I pat the space next to me and shuffle over. He lies down and we stare together and we decide the cloud right above me looks like a rabbit and the one to the left on his side could be a penguin, one of those Emperor penguins standing in the cold, head down, with its egg between its feet. Taller and thinner than Jay's penguin, but I don't say that. I just think it and it makes me happy.

Fifty-two

"It's so pretty," says Molly, turning the bracelet I've given her for her birthday round and round.

"I thought you already had one like that," says Cassie.

"No," she says. "I don't."

Cassie shrugs and blows on her nails. They are pink with a heart on each one.

"I'm not sure these stickers will last," she says. "Did you get cheap ones?"

I shake my head and glare at Cassie.

"What?" she says. "I'm just saying, that's all." She gets up and joins the others outside. Helen has made a really cool mocktail bar with lots of fancy things to put in drinks. We sit and watch them for a bit, waving our hands to let our own nail polish dry. Mine are so great. Light blue with a shiny flower on each.

"At least she and Jess are OK now," says Molly, pointing at the two of them pouring out lemonade. Cassie sticks an umbrella in her drink.

"Those two are always OK in the end," I say.

Ravi shouts that the barbecue is ready and we all gather outside, finding plates and serviettes. There are piles of ribs and burgers and sausages.

"I've done some veggie ones too," says Ravi. I think of Pattie and her plate of '*very vegan*' food and it makes me smile.

Sophia grabs a plate and rushes forward. "Ooh yes, me, please." She sticks her plate out to Ravi. "I'm a vegetarian."

Molly and I share a fond smirk. Sophia is always saying she's a vegetarian. But she has ham in her sarnies for lunch. She always tries to hide the ham under the lettuce.

There are cushions and rugs on the lawn and we sit and eat. One of Cassie's nails has smudged but I don't say anything.

"Have you been away?" says Jess, looking at me.

"Yeah, to my grandparents' for a couple of weeks."

"Nice," says Jess and she blows on her nails, and shows Sophia the rainbow stickers.

I think of Gran and Pops and Jay and how much fun it was.

"Are you still going to Thornberry?" asks Sophia.

"Yep," I say.

"My cousin goes there," says Jess. "She loves it."

"That's good," I say.

"Isn't Jay going to Thornberry too?" says Sophia.

"Yeah," I say. "He is."

"Amy and Jay are *really* good friends now," says Cassie, sucking on her straw, twirling the umbrella round in the glass. "Aren't you, Amy?"

I glare at her over my burger and take a little bite.

"They've spent *loads* of time together," she says.

"How come?" says Jess. The girls are all staring at me now.

I chew my burger, wipe my mouth. "Jay's dad lives opposite my grandparents," I say. "He was there at the same time."

Cassie keeps her mouth on her straw but her eyes flick from one girl to the other.

"She *even* went to his birthday party," she says. She takes the little umbrella from the glass and opens and closes it.

I know what she wants, what she's waiting for.

Sometimes I really don't like Cassie.

Molly goes to speak but she stops. She's not sure what to say. And then Jess says, "That's cool," and I smile at her and she smiles back.

And just like that, thanks to Jess, Cassie's balloon goes *pop*, her game over.

"We're going to miss you *so* much," says Sophia.

"Yeah," says Molly. "But my dad says it can be a good thing, because we'll see each other outside school and just be friends because we love being together."

"A hundred per cent," says Jess. "We'll do tons of stuff."

"Yep," says Molly. "Like the cinema and days out in the holidays."

It sounds good.

Cassie tips her cup on to the grass.

"The lemonade's flat," she says. "I need the loo." She stands up and goes inside, flicking her hair over her shoulders.

Molly pulls herself into me, wraps her arm in mine. "She's finding it the hardest," she says.

"I know," I say. "She always does."

Fifty-three

Mum leans back in the deckchair, giggling away, the phone pressed to her ear.

"He didn't!" she says. "What a thing… OK, Mum, love you. Speak tomorrow." She hangs up. "So funny, Ames," she says. "Gran says after dinner last night Pops counted out the jigsaw pieces. Put them in piles of ten. Got to 998 and made Gran go out with him with the torch and find the last two pieces nestled in the flower beds by the front door!"

"I should hope so," I say, smiling. "We need every single piece."

Mum puts her dinner back on her lap. We are having fish and chips in the garden. Just the five of us, outside in the evening sun.

"I bet you're tired, love, after Molly's party last night."

"I'm fine," I say.

We sit and watch Maxi. He's crawling fast down the

lawn, shrieking as Dad chases him. Every so often he gets to a pile of bricks or rubble and Dad has to scoop him up and set him on a new path.

"I hope you like your room, Ames," says Mum. "I bought all the stuff before we went. Remember I showed you those photos of beds and you sort of half looked and said what you liked."

I smile. "I was annoyed. It felt like you were teasing me a bit. It seemed years away that we could choose stuff."

"As if I'd tease you about that."

I shrug and squeeze more ketchup on my last few chips.

"Wish I'd known," I say. "I'd have paid a bit more attention."

"You said you liked the American look," says Mum.

"I do. I really love it, Mum."

We finish up, scrunch the paper into a ball.

"You done yet, Sam?" says Mum, calling to him. He is down near the bug hotel, watching as he eats. He shakes his head.

"Do you think he'll get bugs in his dinner?" I say. I make a grossed-out face.

"More protein if he does," laughs Mum.

She sits back and looks up at the trees in the garden.

"I like it here," she says. She reaches out for me. "I hope

you will soon, love. I know it's been hard but I want it to be your 'home sweet home.'"

I look at her with slanted eyes. She brushes my cheek.

"We're at about 'home sw—'," I say and she laughs again and says, "I'll take it."

Sam yells. We sit up, look down the garden. Dad is peeling Maxi off the bug hotel. He wriggles and shrieks and one foot catches the top brick and Sam shouts at the top of his voice for Maxi to get lost and go to bed.

"Here we go," I say.

"Shall we dive in the car and go back and help Gran?" giggles Mum and I smile and nod and look up at the sky and watch the clouds. There is nothing interesting. Just a weasel-shaped one and one that reminds me of the candy floss we had at Molly's party. They are light summer clouds but one, just one in the distance, is darker, a deep grey with silver just glinting on the edge of it.

Dad dumps Maxi on my lap.

"Just watch him for a bit, love, will you, while I eat." He reaches for his dinner, wrapped in paper.

Mum passes me Maxi's favourite book, *How Do We Get There?*, and we turn the pages, Maxi poking his fingers through the holes that make the windows of the car and the bus and the rocket. And then he points to the sky and makes a noise like an engine and Mum and Dad collapse into oohing and aahing as if Maxi is the most intelligent baby in the world.

Fifty-four

I wake up to voices in the garden. I can hear Dad and Sam out there already, talking about the plans for the veggie patch. I want to yell at them to be quiet. I turn to my clock. 8.30 a.m. The glow stick from Molly's party is still a faint orange. I roll over and close my eyes. Mum's shouting to Dad to come into the house. She must be about to leave for work. There are footsteps on the stairs, coming up fast. A knock on my door.

"What?" I say, half asleep, irritated, tired.

"It's just me, Ames." Mum opens the door and comes over to the bed and sits down and beams at me. Her face is one big happy smile. It's like the time she told me Dad was coming out of hospital and the time she told me she was pregnant with Maxi. Although we didn't know it was Maxi then. We just knew it was a baby.

"You'll never guess what!" she says, waving her phone in the air. She gets up and turns round in a circle, dancing.

"We've won the lottery," I mutter. "We can move back to the old house."

"Better," she says. I turn to look at her, push my hair off my face.

"What?" I say.

"I just had a phone call," she says.

"Right," I say, dragging it out. "And…"

"It was from the county schools' admissions office. You're in! You have a place at Valley High. I was going to accept it straight away…"

"Did you?" I snap.

"No, I didn't," she says, beaming at me. "I was *about* to and then the very lovely lady said we've got two days to decide. She said we should all talk about it and think carefully and look at all the pros and cons and then phone her on Wednesday."

I nod. And smile. But I'm not sure how I feel.

"You can be with Molly. And Cassie and the others. You see," she says, nudging me, "Dad and I promised and we've kept our promise."

I glare at her a bit. "That's not quite how it's happened, Mum, is it?"

"Oh, I know, but come on, it's great! You've got the school you wanted." She looks at her watch and jumps up. "Got to go! The lab won't wait. Love you, Ames." She kisses me and dashes out. "Help Dad with Maxi, won't you?" she calls as she runs downstairs. "We'll talk about it later."

I lay back and let my mind spin. I'm like Pops. I've borrowed Maxi's spinning top and I've set it off and I've no idea where it will land. I think about Molly and Cassie, Sophia and Jess. I think about Jay and Dana and Summer. The new house, the old house. Gran, Pops. Coins, penguins, basketballs. Around it goes, the colours spinning so fast that they are one big blur.

I stare at the clouds and decide the rabbit is more like a dog but the penguin is still a penguin and I trace the outlines, follow the silvery edge, trying to make the spinning stop.

One Month Later...

"I think it's lovely, Amy," says Gran, smoothing her hands over the blazer. "I'm so pleased you brought it over to show us. Just think, high school tomorrow! Where has the time gone?"

Pops joins us.

"You need shoes on, love," says Gran, staring at his slippers.

"Why?" says Pops.

Gran smiles and strokes his back. "I've told you. We're going over the road for a special surprise. You can't go in your slippers."

"I don't know about that," says Pops and he looks in the mirror and checks his cravat, which he put on this morning. Pops always wears a cravat for special days. He has lots of them, all silky with swirly paisley patterns on them.

It's like he half knows. Like he's almost there.

"You look very smart, Pops," I say.

He nods and then runs his hand over my uniform.

"Who's wearing this then?" he says.

"Me, tomorrow, Pops, for school."

"Hmm," he says.

Gran smiles at me. "We had to wear woollen pleats in my day. So itchy! But this feels lovely." I smile and nod and I'm not sure if it's good or bad that the skirt is smooth and not pleated. I'm not sure one tiny bit any more.

"Right," says Mum, shutting the lounge door behind her, still looking at her phone. "Sorry about that. Bit hard to leave work today but this will be *so* worth it. We'll have to shoot off straight after. I've got a meeting at four." She puts the phone away and checks we are all ready. "So, Dad, you know what we're doing?"

Pops looks in the mirror and examines between his teeth, smooths his cravat.

"Something special," he says.

"Yes, at Paul's house."

"Who's Paul?"

Gran takes his arm and we open the front door. Jay is out front, shooting hoops.

"There's Spinney," says Pops. "Are we going to see Spinney?"

"Yes," says Mum.

"I need something," says Pops. He turns and goes back into the lounge.

"I hope he comes out again," says Gran. She is staring at the 'For Sale' sign, posted by the garden hedge. It just went up this morning.

"You OK about that?" says Mum, nodding at it. "I know it's hard."

Gran pats Mum's arm. "I'm more than OK," she says. "I'm actually really excited. Not sure *you* will be though, with us right round the corner, pestering you all the time."

Mum squeezes her hand. "Pester away," she says.

"It is hard," I say, looking at the sign, linking my arm through Gran's. "Moving house *is* hard. But it's all OK in the end."

Gran pats my hand and says, "Thanks, love, I needed that."

"Right," says Pops, coming out again. "Got it." He leans over to Gran and says to her, "Don't let me forget. I know I forget. I have to give something to Spinney. It's right here." He taps his trouser pocket. "Don't forget to remind me, will you?"

Gran raises her eyebrows and looks at Mum and they smile. "I'll try not to," she says.

We close the front door and cross the road. Me, Mum, Gran and Pops. Just the four of us.

Jay waves and goes round the back calling out, "I'll tell Dad you're here."

"I have my slippers on," says Pops.

"That doesn't matter now," says Gran.

We knock on Jay's door. We wait for a few seconds and then Paul answers.

"Hi, come in. We're all set up!"

We go into the kitchen.

"Gosh, what a beautiful home," says Gran, looking around her. "I need to have a tidy up!"

"I don't know this place," says Pops.

There are footsteps on the stairs, tapping fast. Jay comes in. He has put on his Astros top. Pops' face lights up.

"Spinney Jay!" he says.

"Hi, Pops," says Jay.

We all sit round the kitchen table. There's a vase of flowers and a laptop, slightly open.

"I'm hungry," says Pops. Gran mouths 'sorry' to Paul, but he shakes his head and says, "No worries," and he puts some biscuits on a plate and puts them in front of Pops.

"Yum," says Pops.

"So, Dad," says Mum, slowly and clearly, taking Dad's free hand. "Paul has done something really clever to help us."

"I know," says Pops. "They're delicious. Do you want

one?" He hands the plate to Mum.

"No thanks," says Mum. "Dad, I'm going to tell you again why we're here. You know you talked so much about Spinney and how he went to America and how you lost touch. Well, we gave Paul all the information we had and Paul found him. He's arranged everything. He's going to talk to you very soon." She glances at the clock. "In just a few moments."

"Well, of course he is," says Pops, laughing, pointing at Paul. "He's right there. That man you just said. He has *lovely* biscuits."

"No, *Spinney*, Dad. Jerry Spinneyfields. *He's* going to talk to you."

I'm not sure this is going to work.

"Spinney," says Pops. "He went to America."

"Yes, I know, Dad. But Paul found him. He's in America still, but he's going to talk to you on the screen."

"Oh," says Pops. "Have you tried these?" He holds up a biscuit. "They have raisins in them." He picks a raisin out and shows her.

"We'll just have to see," mutters Mum.

The computer makes a pinging noise and Paul presses a few buttons and moves the screen so we can all see it. Pops leans in, watches. He goes to take a bite of his biscuit but he stops, the biscuit in mid-air, and puts it down again. He touches the screen, very gently. Mum leans forward, ready to pull his hand back, worried about the greasy fingermarks but Paul stops her, shakes his head and mouths that it's fine. I like the way Paul does that.

"Well, I never," says Pops. "Spinney, my old chap. Is that you?" He turns round to Gran. "Suzie, Suzie, look who it is! Spinney." And then he bounces a little in his chair and Gran puts an arm on his shoulder as if to calm him.

"Yes, it's him," she says.

Spinney smiles and says, "Terry, my old mucker, look how well you are!"

"Oh, I'm not really," says Pops. "You've lost your hair, Spinney!"

"You haven't, Terry. Same old thick mop!" Pops pulls one hand through his hair, tugs it a little.

"Oh my God," says Paul, very quietly. "Spinney is *so* like Jay. I get it now." He wraps his arm around Jay and hugs him.

"Is that your family there?" asks Spinney.

"Yes," says Pops. "This is my daughter Julie and my granddaughter Amy." He beckons us over to say hello. "And Suzie of course, you remember Suzie."

Spinney waves and smiles.

Mum talks about Sam and Maxi and Dad and how everyone says, '*Hello*,' and hopes to see Spinney again.

"Sounds great," says Spinney. "Now, Terry, I want you to meet someone, my special someone." A man joins him, lays one hand on his shoulder. "This is Frank."

"Hey, guys!" says Frank. "It's a pleasure to meet y'all." Frank has a very strong American accent. Pops leans in closer again. He touches the screen with one finger, first on Spinney's face and then on Frank's.

"Well, I never," says Pops. "What an honour to meet you, Frank. You taken on the old Spinney?"

Frank bursts out laughing. He laughs so hard that we all laugh too, joining in the fun.

"I've put up with him for twenty-three years," says Frank. He says twenty with no 't' sound so it's just 'twenny'. It sounds so cool.

"That's a long time," says Pops. "We've been playing a bit of shove ha'penny, me and young…" He forgets Jay's name. He looks round to find him. Jay moves closer.

"With me! Hi, I-I'm Jay. Spinney Jay, he calls me!"

"That's right," says Pops. "Been showing him how to shift those coins. He's a natural."

Spinney claps his hands in joy. "Been a few years, that has, Terry. I hope you've beaten him, Jay!"

Jay goes to speak. Stops. We wait. Pops looks at Jay and smiles, very gently. He knows to wait. He has remembered.

"I-I have!" says Jay. "Just a few times."

They tell stories, share memories, remembering the games and the boards and the famous loss to another pub that had an old bog oak board. Spinney tells a great story of Pops winning the pub championship.

"Yes," says Pops. "And I had to drink a half gallon of beer as the prize! Never been so ill."

"It's all crystal clear," whispers Gran.

They talk families and old work mates. Pops nibbles on his biscuit, staring at Spinney, reliving the days of the past. Captain wanders in and Jay scoops him up. He comes and stands with me and I tickle Captain under his chin.

And then Spinney talks about his life with Frank and their friends and travel and Pops can't hold on. It's like the top has started to spin and he's trying to pin it to one point and he can't.

"Not long left," says Paul, checking the screen. "Forty-five minutes, these calls." Mum nods and says quietly to Paul, "Yes, I think Dad's tired now." She turns back to Pops and Spinney.

"We'll have to say goodbye soon," says Mum. "Time is running out."

Pops sits back. "Yes, it is," he says. "Time is short." He reaches out again, touches Spinney's face and then Frank's.

It's like by touching the glass, the spinning stops.

Spinney leans forward. "I want to tell your family something," he says. "Your dad, your pops, he gave me an incredible friendship you know, all those years ago." He sniffs hard, his mouth twists a little. Frank puts one arm on his back. "After our apprenticeship, things were tough for me. But your dad, your pops, was *always* there."

And then Pops says, very quietly, "*Spinner, the winner, Spinner, my friend…*"

And Spinney finishes the line, "*Spinney and Terry, chums 'til the end.*"

Gran lays her hand on Pops' shoulder. Jay looks at me and smiles and I smile back, lift a hand to stroke Captain's head.

Spinney waves and then his face is snapped away.

We are all very quiet. Paul takes the laptop and shuts it down.

"Well, I never," says Pops, taking another biscuit. "Incredible. Did you see?" he asks, turning round to us all. "Did you?"

"We did," says Mum, hugging him tight. "Thanks so much, Paul."

We head out to the hall. Pops stops by the door, turns and looks straight at Paul.

"Thank you," he says.

"You're so welcome," says Paul. "It was a pleasure."

"That was the nicest biscuit I've ever had," says Pops.

"I'm glad," says Paul, smiling.

"Oh gosh," says Gran, lifting one hand to her face. "Terry love, you had something for Spinney, in your pocket."

"Did I?" says Pops.

"Yes, in your pocket," says Gran. "I forgot."

Pops tuts. "You did," he says. "Look at you, being all forgetful." He smiles at Gran and for a second he is teasing her just like he used to. Gran feels it too.

"Yes, look at me, all forgetful." She smiles at him and says, "Check your pocket."

Pops puts his hands in both pockets and pulls out a piece of paper.

"I have this," he says, "for Spinney Jay."

Jay puts Captain down and reaches for the paper.

"The rules," says Pops. "I wrote them down for you. As me and Spinney played. Might be different to some rules but that's how we always played. I wrote them down so you don't forget. So you always remember."

Jay folds out the paper. He looks up at Pops.

"Thank you," he says. His eyes are wide. He looks down again at the sheet.

Pops nods and turns and he crosses the road, holding Gran's arm, his slippers just missing a giant puddle in the middle of the road.

I turn back and wave at Jay.

"See you soon," I say. "Have fun tomorrow!"

He gives me a thumbs up, puts the paper down on the hall table and fetches his basketball, runs with it and then turns and shoots and scores a perfect hoop.

The Next Day

The bus stop is busy. Nobody I know gets on here. Little groups chat and shout. I stare down the road, watching for the bus. The tiny amount of cereal I managed to choke down might come back up at any minute. I pull at my skirt for the tenth time, worry that my tie is tied too big, too small, too tight.

My phone pings. It's Molly.

So glad I'm seeing u today 😄

I smile. I will see her. And I'm glad.

I'm about to reply when the bus comes round the corner. I put my phone in my inside pocket, zip it up. The other kids pick up their bags, shuffle forward. A couple of older lads are pushing each other and laughing. Their ties are very loose and low. I pull mine a bit, wiggle it looser from its knot. The bus stops and I climb the steps.

"Year Sevens at the front, please," says the driver, smiling.

"Good to see you, rabble! Older ones to the rear. Sit down quickly, please. Glad to see you came back, Levi!"

I think Levi is just in front of me. He is very, very tall.

"Course I did, Babs. Couldn't wait for one last year to ride the fun machine again!"

"Lying toad!" Babs laughs and Levi bounces on to the bus. I follow him on. He's in his last year. I feel shiny new.

"Morning," says Babs, smiling at me. "On you get."

There are no spaces at the front. I start to feel a little hot. And then I hear a voice.

"Amy, here, I saved you one!" I look up and at first I don't recognize her. The purple streak has gone. She pats the seat next to her, by the window. I squeeze past and sit next to Summer.

"You didn't get one either!" she says, pointing to my skirt. I shake my head. "Apparently only half the year managed to. That's what Dana thinks anyway."

"I'm so glad," I say.

"Me too," says Summer. "I literally was so cross with my mum. I thought I'd be the only one not in the right skirt!"

Someone in the seat behind shouts her name and Summer turns to talk to him. I glance round at the other girls. Some have green-and-blue pleated skirts but I can see plain green ones like ours too.

I take out my phone and reply to Molly.

> **Thanks for inviting me later** 😊
> **Can't wait. Will be good to see**
> **Sophia and Cassie 2. Hope u have a**
> **great day. I'm on the bus. U ok?**

I wait a few seconds and she replies with three hearts and a big thumbs up. And then she puts:

> **On bus 2. Cass wont shut up** 👀

I put my phone away and look out of the window and smile a little. I can just imagine Cassie chatting away, digging in her bag, dropping her things. Some things about Cassie will never change. But other things between me and Cassie have changed a lot. And I'm glad.

Summer spins back and asks if I've brought snacks with me and I shake my head and she offers me one of hers.

"I liked your purple hair," I say.

"Thanks!" says Summer. "I'm thinking of bright red for Christmas."

The bus turns into the high school gates. I look out of the window and the first person I see is Jay. He's walking in with a friend. Maybe it's Ben. I lean round. He sees me. He raises one hand and smiles.

I look up at the sky and catch a glimpse of a white cloud,

drifting past quite fast, pulled as it goes, stretching out, and it reminds me so much of Maxi's giraffe. I rummage in my pocket, find my phone to take a photo but when I look up the cloud has changed, the giraffe neck now just a mass of white cloud, tumbling by in the wind.

The bus pulls up next to the school and there is no sky now, just a large brick wall and a row of classroom windows.

I hug my bag close and feel as ready as I'm ever going to be.

RULES OF SHOVE HA'PENNY
FOR SPINNEY JAY

THE GAME

A board game for two players who attempt
to shove ha'pennies down a board trying
to get them into marked 'beds'.

THE BOARD

About 24 x 13 inches, with a lip that hooks on to
the end of the table. There are nine 'beds' marked
across the middle, each about 1 inch wide. Each
bed is separated from the next by a narrow groove.
At the edge of each bed is a black area used for
marking the number of successful ha'pennies that
have landed in that bed. They are marked at the
end of each go with chalk by the opponent.

HOW TO PLAY

A player puts a ha'penny at the front of the board with about a quarter of its width overlapping the edge. The player shoves this with the side of his hand and starts by trying to put a coin in the first bed. Then the player tries to fill each further bed.

Each 'go' consists of shoving five coins. Those which go into a bed may be brought back and used again (after the chalk mark is made so you don't forget!).

The 'go' ends when no further coins are in a bed.

If a coin goes past the bottom bed it is withdrawn by the opponent and cannot be used again in that go. If the coin is lying over the edge of a bed, it can be used for other coins to knock against and find a bed (see below).

The aim is to get three ha'penny coins in each lane. So each section at the side of the bed needs three chalk marks. If you get a fourth coin in the lane, this is a foul and your opponent gets the mark!

USEFUL THINGS TO KNOW

A BUILD — This is a usefully placed ha'penny, which has its edge just overlapping the back edge of a bed. This can be of great help to the next coin — it can collide with it and thus go into a bed.

A FLOAT — This is a ha'penny coin, which is 'shoved' into a bed at the first attempt without the aid of a build. These are very valuable — a float to one of the last beds is very rare! (Seen you do it twice, Spinney Jay!)

THE PERFECT GO! — This is when all beds are filled in one go! This is very hard to do. I've done it once in my whole life!

TIPS — Use talc powder on the board. Sprinkle it and rub it down with a soft cloth. It helps to fill any cracks and keep the board smooth! And rub the coin on the board before your go to take the dust away and get things smooth.

DISPUTES! — Some boards have fancy metal strips that are brought down to check if the coin is over the line — I've never had a board like this — we just have to decide together if the coin is clear of the line! Sometimes you need to ask someone else to adjudicate!

People have different rules but this is how me and Spinney played!

Have fun, Spinney Jay — you're a natural-born player!

Pops

Acknowledgements

As always, my agent Gill McLay comes first – thank you for your years of belief and encouragement. Ella Whiddett, editor extraordinaire – when we first met with Ruth, Gill and Lauren, you mentioned a book about siblings and from that comment I bounced back to Amy and Jay who once existed in a very different guise! From there, *Every Cloud* was born and it has been the most fantastic journey working with you to find dear Amy's path.

I have so much appreciation for the amazing team at Stripes – Lauren Ace and crew – you are fab!

So much of this book is about family and friendship and for that I have been truly blessed. Nick and the boys and my precious extended family – thank you always. Mum – your voice weaves through this story and how I wish you could now be a part of the journey. Dad – your shove ha'penny help was essential and the hours you have played with the boys set me up well. Friends – well, what can I say? A lifetime of friendship from my precious fruits whose encouragement and love has always guided me – how my confidence grew after our first Digger reading round the fire! You are always there for me and I love you so for it.

Kate, Sam, Ella H, Alex – thank you so much for your honesty and help with this book.

Lastly to Freddie – thanks for being my best reader and most of all, for being you.

About the author

Ros Roberts lives in the north of England with her husband and family. She writes in her shed and loves to create stories and poems about everyday things. Ros used to teach and now she is privileged to be able to help young people to write creatively – free writing is dear to her heart. Ros loves tennis, brunch, TV and she is a proud pluviophile – a lover of the rain! She loves dogs too – her Bernese mountain dog Texi inspired her first children's book, *Digger and Me*.

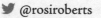 @rosiroberts ⬛ @rosrobertswriter